MODERN MADNESS

PRAISE FOR TIM CHIZMAR

"Tim Chizmar reaches past the conventions of the commonplace and holds nothing back!"

— CLIVE BARKER, MASTER OF HORROR AND THE CREATOR OF *HELLRAISER*, *LORD OF ILLUSIONS*, *NIGHTBREED*, *CANDYMAN*, ETC.

"Tim Chizmar, as witnesses will agree, is nearly as terrifying as his writings. Nearly."

— *FANGORIA MAGAZINE*

"I knew I had a long-lost horror loving cousin somewhere out there in the world ... and I think I just found him. Tim Chizmar — What! No relation, you say? He is now on my short list of new authors to look for! His stories are bizarre and scary and sizzle with raw energy. Check him out!"

— RICHARD CHIZMAR, EDITOR AT *CEMETERY DANCE MAGAZINE* & CO-AUTHOR (WITH STEPHEN KING) FOR *NEW YORK TIMES* BESTSELLING *GWENDY'S BUTTON BOX*

"The danger of reading horror fiction is that you never know what's lurking on that next page. Like the protagonists in the stories themselves, any moment you could find your boundaries stretched, cracked, or ripped asunder. And so, I have to advise you not to read the work of Tim Chizmar because I can guarantee that it will melt your face off with sheer awesomeness. If you're okay with being faceless, then please read on. In my opinion, it's a good tradeoff."

— BRAD C. HODSON, AUTHOR OF *THE MUD ANGEL*

"Tim Chizmar brings a unique blend of humor, heart, and horror to his stories, taking the reader on an odyssey through his warped and creative imagination. Buckle up and enjoy the ride."

— S. G. BROWNE, AUTHOR OF *BREATHERS* & *LUCKY BASTARD*

"Tim Chizmar's writing bristles with a barely harnessed energy, threatening to break free and run wild at any moment. It feels dangerous, like driving fast down the freeway against traffic. It seems like it could go wrong at any moment, but the story arrives intact to a satisfying and often surprising conclusion."

— IAN WELKE, AUTHOR OF *THE WHISPERER IN DISSONANCE*
& *END TIMES AT RIDGEMONT HIGH*

"Chizmar's talent is for writing characters who demand your attention, pulling you into their stories and the horrific journeys they go through. His ability to write realistic dialogue in an extraordinarily haunting way sets him far apart from a lot of today's writers. Hands down, one of the most entertaining and colorful up-and-coming authors in the genre, Tim is someone to watch, as it's apparent that he'll be around for a long, LONG time."

— JERRY SMITH, EDITOR-IN-CHIEF AT *ICONS OF FRIGHT*,
FREELANCE WRITER/*FANGORIA, DELIRIUM MAGAZINE*,
SCREENWRITER FOR *VARMINT*

"Tim Chizmar's writing is deliciously bizarre and macabre; he tells haunting stories loaded with irony."

— D.H. JONATHAN, AUTHOR OF *THE VOLUNTEER*

"Tim Chizmar is a whirlwind of imagination, energy, and madness—and the stories he writes are every bit as imaginative, energetic, and mad as the man himself."

— MARTIN LASTRAPES, AUTHOR OF *THE VAMPIRE AND THE HUNTER* TRILOGY AND *INSIDE THE OUTSIDE*

"Tim Chizmar proves an impressive talent in genre fiction, an emerging voice that is heard as equal parts wit, insight, and artistry."

— ERIC J. GUIGNARD, *BRAM STOKER AWARD*-WINNER & FINALIST FOR *INTERNATIONAL THRILLER WRITERS* AWARD

"Tim Chizmar's work speaks for itself... in a high-pitched Banshee wail that chills the soul, rattles your teeth, and flays the living flesh from your quivering bones. And he somehow managed this with a wry, twisted humor that makes you laugh nervously as you piss your pants in fright! Great stuff!"

— JERYD POJAWA, Two-time *Academy Award*-winning art director, *The Abyss* and *Terminator 2*

"Tim Chizmar is on my bucket list. I want to kill him with a bucket... the one I vomited into violently after reading stories so terrifying that I literally pulled out my eyes and stuck them in my ass, so I could watch as I shit myself. Chizmar's writing well cause permamintt brian dalmedgee."

— ROBERT CORPSY RHINE, Deaditor-In-Chief of *Girls and Corpses Magazine*

"Tim is the quintessential evil clown. A natural story weaver, a yarn spinner-but beware his faux-friendly demeanor! Don't get drawn in when he flashes that smile. Look closer and see the dark, twisted glint in his eye for it is here that he will capture your soul. If you choose to follow him down the rabbit hole into his sick, maddening world, you must do so gladly for you may never return. If you love horrible things, you will love Tim Chizmar!"

— KATARINA LEIGH WATERS, *WWE* diva, and story contributor to *Hell Comes to Hollywood 2*

"Tim Chizmar has a talent for drawing in his audience of readers or listeners, fascinating them with horror or comedy or both, and sending them away full of enthusiasm to encounter more of his work. I don't know anyone with a more dramatic talent for situating horror in everyday settings in a completely believable way. If you're looking for a way to lose sleep, if you enjoy surprises that you never saw coming, if you love creativity, read Tim Chizmar!"

— Laura L Mays Hoopes, Professor of Molecular Biology and Author of *Breaking Through the Spiral Ceiling, An American Woman Becomes a DNA Scientist.*

ALSO BY TIM CHIZMAR

Modern Madness 2: The Screaming Virgins

Soul Traitor

Also Featured in:

18 Wheels of Horror

Hell Comes to Hollywood 2

Chicken Soup for the Soul: Random Acts of Kindness

Halloween Tales

A Valley of Light and Shadow: Las Vegas Writers on good and evil

It's Alive: Bringing your Nightmares to Life

MODERN MADNESS

GATEWAY TO THE GROTESQUE
SECOND EDITION

TIM CHIZMAR

MODERN MADNESS: Gateway to the Grotesque - 2nd Edition

Copyright © 2020 by Timothy C. Chizmar.

Cover Copyright © 2020 by Timothy C. Chizmar

All Rights Reserved.

Cover Design Edits by Stacey

Editing services provided by Edits by Stacey

LIBBY originally printed in HELL COMES TO HOLLYWOOD 2

FARKELBERRY FORREST CEMETERY originally printed in HALLOWEEN TALES

CARGO originally printed in 18 WHEELS OF HORROR

Originally titled WRESTLING WITH EVIL, Published as LET'S GET READY TO LET THE HEADS ROLL in *Fangoria Magazine* Issue 345 Released Nov. 2015 Cowritten by John Palisano

AT THE FEET OF THE MASTER - INTERVIEW WITH CLIVE BARKER Originally published in the HWA Bram Stoker award winning collection *It's Alive: Bringing Your Nightmares to Life*, Edited by Joe Mynhardt and published by Crystal Lake Publishing.

ISBN: digital 978-1-949318-46-3

Paperback 978-1-949318-47-0

Hardcover 978-1-949318-48-7

Work submitted to the Library of Congress

Published by SpookyNinjaKitty @ Spookyninjakitty.com

This is a work of fiction, no resemblance to persons
living or dead was intended by the author. Thank you for supporting art.

CONTENTS

"If you're going to be CRAZY. You have to get paid for it or else you're going to be locked up."

— HUNTER S. THOMPSON

INTRODUCTION

Hello Reader,

Let's just be honest, I know I already like you. -I might even love you; I've been watching you for a while and I can tell you got damn good taste in books, or at least in writers, that's for sure. However, in this instance you may have bit off more than you can chew. I'm a little worried about you; you see, not everyone can handle this epic madness and trust me, this madness was not created for everyone. The team at SpookyNinjaKitty sent out ten copies to supposed horror fans for feedback, and by the very next day, six had dropped dead of heart attacks, three committed suicide, and the last one has never been seen again. I just got a letter from him recently with alphabet letters cut from magazines spelling out something about needing to stop me before I bring about the coming of a Dark Lord. I think that means he liked it. Fans, ya know, I can never tell with them!

Anyway, like many normal people, I too have a comfort zone I'm afraid to leave. In my case, it is in my writing career. I'm very comfy within the realms of screenwriting, magazine articles, ghostwriting, and even banging out short stories. Anytime, anywhere I can take on a project or idea and wham! Bam! I knock it out to the expectations of the buyer and myself, for the most part, but I'm feeling a tug on my soul to dare step over the line of comfort into a whole new dimension of crazy, full-length novels. This even scares me, dear reader. So, in many ways this book you are holding is my gateway drug; what you are reading is my first attempt to collect my smaller various crazy bits and pieces into an original collection. Don't be fooled though, short can still be deadly. A bullet isn't very big, but it'll blow a hole through your guts spilling them all over your kitchen counter. Poison even in small doses will still kill Grandpa when he sips his soup. Are these tales any good? Is it art? Maybe it's just plain 'ol pure madness in the form of words spewed on a page waiting to infect your delicate brain tissues, and for that being the case . . . good. I'll call that a success. Life can be mundane and boring; let my crazy wash over you. My work is not for the uptight or even in most cases the sane, but if you are a fan of the weird, the wild, the disturbed, and the freaky, well then, you may have a good time.

To get to this point, I have many people to thank, and I will- goddammit -just hold your horses that comes much later. First, let's see if you'll enjoy reading the thing. I've been motivated and encouraged by my kindred spirits, the writer friends and fellow creative thinkers that dwell in organizations such as the Horror Writers Association, Idaho Writers Guild, California Writers Club, and the amazing people I'm met lurking in outrageous costumes at various horror conventions and comic-cons all over the globe. It has been my pleasure to get to know you twisted souls and hopefully offer you encouragement to chase your crazy dreams just as I'm doing right now.

I cannot say if my ART is good or bad; it simply IS. I didn't write it for me. I wrote it because they were stories on my heart to be released. If you like them, then perhaps it was always meant for you, so ultimately, you'll be the judge of the quality. But I hope you enjoy this as much as I enjoyed birthing it into the world through my hands. It was a messy birth and many of its siblings did not survive; I cleaned off most of the blood. So, rock it gently in your arms... I think it has your eyes.

In this collection, you will see only the finest in old ladies terrorized by spiders, fame-seeking wannabe actors in search of the Mexican macabre, hot young teenagers making nookie in a cemetery, an incarcerated demon on death row in Hell, and much more. Some of these stories have appeared in other collections and some have never been seen before now; they were locked away behind vaults of protective metal. Today they have been scattered to the winds in search of you, and among the craziness there is an adaptation from a feature length screenplay I co-wrote back in 2011 with a twisted fella named Kevin Lahaie. Seriously, he scares the shit outta me, and I love that about him. It tells a story about what may in fact go on behind the gates of a family nudist resort. Spoiler alert: some people die horribly all while being totally buck ass naked.

What's wrong with you that you'll read this kinda stuff? Wait, what's *wrong with me* that I wrote it? Both my parents are indeed convicted felons, so there's that, but we'll get into that another time in another place, my memoir perhaps. Before we embark, let me share a brief glimpse at my youth. When I was a child, I lost myself in dark, disturbed, and scary books. One day, a morally righteous librarian refused to let me take out the books. Reading about demons, be-headings, and cannibalism wasn't the norm in the small town of Linesville, Pennsylvania. When I brought my mother down there to confront the self-appointed censor, my mother insisted that I be allowed to read "WHATEVER BOOKS I WANTED." This upset the librarian. So, she looked my mother in the eye and said in front of my young impressionable self, "I will warn you now that your son is going to grow up to be a great horror writer one day... OR A SERIAL KILLER." So yeah, now is a good time to mention that as of this writing, I haven't killed anyone, YET. The day's not over, and there's a neighbor getting on my nerves, but yeah... I've written and sold many screenplays in Hollywood. What really drives my success (if you want to call it that) is my understanding that somewhere in Pennsylvania a librarian is still praying for my soul.

1

———

UNLOCKING THE DOOR

The grotesquely elegant gathered together in thunderous approval, empathy, and love. All cloaked figures beyond the realms of understanding were present at the joyous occasion. The entities danced and spun openly, embracing the moonlight. It was not every day that the Count took a companion to be his bride in the forever night. He stepped out of the complete shadows and glided over to her, his right arm outstretched, reaching as splinters of shadows danced all around. The bronze skinned, eighteen-year-old robust girl had dreamed of this moment all her young life; she eagerly put her hand into his, and ancient claws tightened its grip in response. Their eyes locked in an eternal understanding and she turned her neck towards his eager mouth; the voyeurs murmured in agreement. She leaned in, closing her eyes... waiting for Dracula's kiss...

"Amaya." She squinted her eyes at the sound of her name. It wasn't her master's voice she was hearing.

The vampire's mouth opened with a glimmer of perfectly shaped snake-like fangs waiting to snap on her jugular, but then... she heard it again...

"Amaya," the angry voice called. The cranky old lady hollered again, "Get over here this instant, you daft girl. Customers are waiting." The girl shook herself fully from her fantasy. She screamed out loud in frustration and glared in the direction of the shrill voice calling to her. Customers were always waiting at The Majik Shoppe. Amaya's grandmother, Draga Mizelli, had run this establishment for what felt to her like a million years. Amaya lit up a cigarette, took a puff, and watched as an underage girl with her baby in a stroller begged for coins. She walked the cigarette over and gave it to the young mom, then stormed her way over to the front of the tiny shop to the wrinkled chubby lady waiting for her. This walking relic wore colored fabrics and gaudy jewelry; she pulled her granddaughter in close to her bosom; as she did, her jewelry made jingle jangle sounds.

"What was it this time pulling you away?" Draga poked the dream weaver in her left shoulder as she continued, "Were zombies eating what's left of your brains?"

"No, this time I was the bride of Dracula."

"Dracula," the old lady laughed. "You're the only girl I know that dreams of darkness while being in the sunshine. You bengalia, I tell you over and over and over again that your daydreams won't fill the champagne glass, so get over there and sell to the marks. Please, please, please, try some tarot this time, enough with these belly dancing classes." Amaya humored this position as an assistant at the shop but knew it's not where she was meant to be long term. One day she would escape all of this; her grandmother, who had cared for her, was still just a liability to her future. Something was watching her; Amaya felt it and knew that one day the opportunity would present itself for her to join the other dark souled ones that never fit into this world. Until then, she would humor the old woman.

She spun the girl around and pushed her towards the two females reading the sign. The sign read like a menu, but not for Roma stews and sandwiches; rather it listed all the fantastical experiences one could have at The Majik Shoppe, for the right price of course. Besides the usual Gypsy flair of tarot and palm readings, tea leaves, formulations, conjuring of spirits for either blessings or curses; the shop also offered unique pieces that Draga created. She tendered life and career roadmaps or teachings of astral projection through regular meditation, and many more services. They also had t-shirts, mugs, oils, incense, elixirs, powders, and the like to grab on the way out. All these mementos had printed the business address of The Majik Shoppe on it. Tourists loved it. Amaya grabbed some silk, wrapped it around her waist to appear more gypsy and less Romani and quickly walked up to the two blondes, who were obviously American tourists.

"Oh my gawd, are you a real Gypsy?" exclaimed one blonde. "Like for reals?" Amaya nodded.

"This is so cool, all of this." The American waved her hands with the painted pink nails all over the signage. "But you already know that, right?"

The pink nailed girlfriend was wearing a bright yellow t-shirt with "I HEART LA" written on it. She chimed in, "We love the culture here and are both super interested in becoming famous belly dancers."

Amaya knew what her grandmother had said, so she started a routine that led to more psychic readings. It was called The Rings Routine... "Okay, sure belly dancing is fun; I can get into that with you, but first let me ask you do you always wear your rings like that?"

"Well, yeah, why?" Both girls leaned in, eager to hear the secrets that this mysterious girl would share.

"Oh, no reason. It's just that where you place your rings on your hand says a lot about your future..." The girls were completely fascinated, wanting to know more.

Both girls were captivated at the age-old Rings Routine con. It comprised basic cold readings and taking for granted that this young girl half their age suddenly knew ancient secrets to unlock their intimate futures. Amaya had seen this many times before. She was a pro. Moments later, seated around a magic crystal ball, tarot cards were spread on the table. Amaya read the fortune for the girls. She expected to let her words flow; she spun predictions of traditional happy lives, attractive husbands and children, wealth and fame, and all the other bullshit these Americans like to hear proclaimed aloud. But then something changed. The air got thick all around and the smell of charcoal was in her nose. A small door appeared on the far wall behind the tourists. At first Amaya tried to go through the motions, and ignored it, but it distracted her. She rushed through the session and led the girls out but not hesitating to stop briefly and sell them some Majik Shoppe merchandise before closing up the shop in order to inspect this new development.

Amaya knew this had never been here before. Could this be the entrance she'd waited for her whole life? The invitation to the darkness was finally within her grasp. She got on the floor and looked it all over, her brown eyes taking in every detail in the black wood. Etchings and carvings depicted humans in various stages of both ecstasy and torment; simultaneous pleasures and pain in evidence of years of bargains made. The door could not be opened without unlocking an old rusted lock that hung in opposition to her curiosity. She was so engrossed in tugging on it she missed the arrival of Draga behind her now with a long broom.

"Oh, piss! Get away from that damned thing, you bengalia," The overprotective grandmother hollered as she swatted at her granddaughter's head. "You need to leave shop right now. There's nothing for you here."

"No, I can't leave grandmother- this is the coolest thing that has ever happened to me. A tiny gateway just appeared out of nowhere, I gotta know what this is about."

"It's nothing and should stay that way. We added it yesterday to keep jars on. See nothing special for your eyes."

"That's not true." Amaya took the sweeping tool from the older lady's hands. "Tell me the truth and I'll leave it alone." Draga Mizelli sized up her grandchild's curiosity, then turned her back to open a brown glass bottle. Draga hardly drank, but knew that liqueur would only ease her honesty. The exasperated old lady drug one of the red velvet chairs to separate Amaya from her newly discovered door and sat on it, blocking her view.

"Fine, I know everything about this door." She took a swig from the hooch. "This gateway belongs to the Butyanko." She had her granddaughter's full attention for the first time in perhaps ever. "I don't even like saying his name, but that is him." She whispered and pointed to the locked-up doorway. "Your ancestors assisted some creature of darkness and as a reward it has anointed our family with…" She paused for more drink to calm her nerves. "A blessing on each new generation family as they reach maturity; now it comes to you Amaya, but you must listen to me. This has been a curse on the family, not a blessing. Whatever deals were made, starting with the brothers Yarb and Tobbar ages ago with the dark entity, Butyanko, have been twisted over the years, and nobody has ever lived happily ever after." She grabbed her granddaughter's shoulders to emphasize her point, "Nobody."

Amaya nodded with her mouth hung open, thinking of the possibilities this could provide her with.

"I can see you're all hyped up, well stop it. No good comes from it. I dealt with the little prick and it promised to get my family to America. They got there but as you know they were killed getting off the boat." She waved the bottle toward the framed family pictures on the wall. "Then there's the case of my daughter - your mother…"

Amaya had heard of her mother's suicide, but not why she would make such a decision to leave a young child alone without a parent.

"Your ma wanted nothing more in the world than to be a mother, so much so that she only asked for one thing of the Butyanko. A healthy baby. You. You were her wish."

"Well, then…" The young girl swirled this information in her mind. "Then why'd she leave me?"

"Kaka rocka nixis bengalia." Amaya hated when she only spoke in Romani, but she waited as was asked to do. "Maybe we talk about this tomorrow."

"No. I need to know or I'll go away with it tonight, far away." The two sat in proximity but eons of wisdom and knowledge apart. Draga hoped she could get through to her before it was too late.

"Your mother slowly grew to resent that her baby was put in her by the black arts and not by love. Not even by a man's touch. You see your ma wasn't attractive that's why I don't hang her pictures up; she had no hope for love. Your mother was a virgin up to her jumping off the high wall of Bran Castle." This struck Amaya hard, and she felt a deep sense of regret for her mother's lot in life. She hadn't chosen to be born ugly and in a dirt-poor gypsy family. "So, you see many of our ancestors regretted using this because the little bastard is a trickster god. If you're not careful, it will use your own words against you." Looking deep into Amaya's big brown eyes she continued, "It will cause your demise, gleefully."

"Okay, but how do I open the lock?"

"You don't. Not tonight, not next Christmas, not ever."

"I won't do it. I have to know." Amaya Mizelli stared long and hard at her only living blood relative. "Please."

"It opens with the blood of something you loved smeared on it, I used a chicken, and your mother used a pig. It has to be something that the person has strong emotions for, not just a random thing. You had to truly care about it, even a little bit will do it."

"Oh." Amaya had never hurt anything. Freaky dreams of monsters and death invaded her thoughts, but in the real world she'd been a vanilla girl. She took all this information in. "On the upside though, with all this, I can get a wish granted. In that way, Grandma, he's like my personal Genie in a lamp."

"More like a Jinn," the elder lady grunted thinking of her own encounters and taking another slurp of the bottle. The old woman's eyes began to glaze over and drop tears that ran lines over the crevices in her plump face. "The ritual of Butyanko must never be done, you're not to try to outsmart him. The door showed up. The door can stay locked there. It's calling to you, yes, but you don't have to do what others did." She hoped sincerely these words made the true impact; a lifesaving impact on the family legacy and future. "I've done all I can for you." She got up from the chair. "I pray you do the right thing. You're the last of the Mizelli family. I call you bengalia sometimes, but I don't mean it- if you ever go in there, talk with him, then you are a female idiot for real."

"I heard you. I understand." Amaya stood from her position sitting on the floor and put her hand on the old woman's shoulder. "I know exactly what to ask for. I won't squander it, it's my birthright and I'm going to get it right." Draga smirked a half-heartedly, not knowing where this was going but hoping she got through to the girl.

Amaya took a deep breath and proudly announced, "I will become a vampire tonight!" She waited for the hugs and excitement to come from her plump, colorful old matriarch. It never came. What did come fast and hard was a slap that knocked Amaya back. She looked on in complete shock as her grandmother's tearful face now filled rage never before seen.

"Fool, I'm ashamed of you. You embarrass me, you embarrass everyone! What is wrong with you? Vampires and ghouls and shit always coming out of your mouth; there's no such thing, and I'll be damned if I let you screw up your one shot at a better life. I'd rather you ignore the door, but if you won't..." She set the bottle down on the crystal ball table, knocking over some candles. "If you won't then please listen, this is your chance to get out of the squalor, maybe settle in Braddock, Pennsylvania with the other successful Roma. Go someplace that is not highlighted on the map for sex trafficking, forced labor and begging. Have you looked around where we live–this dump of a land?"

Amaya held her right hand to her still red cheek. It still stung from the surprise attack by her intoxicated grandma. "You're right- I do deserve a better life than this." For the first time in a long time, the two women agreed. Draga helped her to her feet and wrapped her arms around her, pulling her in close. Amaya slipped her hand into her dress pocket; there she fumbled with a tool her grandmother had bought her on her sixteenth birthday. It was purchased to protect her in times of an emergency. She gripped the knife, settled in the sheath attached to it from her waist. The first thrust at Draga didn't penetrate completely but only tore fabric and got a surprised look on her face. The second swipe cut into the old woman's meat. After that, it all became a blur. She couldn't stop watching it slide in and out of her flesh as the elder woman crumpled in a heap with her left arm outstretched. Blood rained on the area in front of the tiny door as though a Hollywood red carpet event extending itself in a greeting to a better life. The blood that stayed on Amaya's hands seemed to glow neon in the light of the red lamps in The Majik Shoppe.

"What a waste, you dumb girl, vampires aren't real." Draga Mizelli gurgled on blood spitting it up on her face which now was a crimson mask; she suffocated as her lungs filled with blood. Amaya had never seen her grandmother look so lovely. This had to happen; she knew it had been her eventuality in life, to be sacrificed for her granddaughter's uprising. Finally, it was all coming together.

"Well, then what about demons and curses, you old hag." Amaya's mind reeled with the thoughts of the cloaked ones applauding her with Dracula calling to his future bride that he would be with her soon. She sat there looking at the scene, how otherworldly it all seemed with the old dead body, the knife still in her hand and the blood, the blood was everywhere. It had ruined one of her few good dresses. The tiny black door with its black lock was there in the distance. As if in a daze, Amaya went to it. She knew how to open it. Laying her right palm on the lock with Draga's blood forming a warm bond between her flesh and the rusty steel, the lock popped open on its own. She stepped back to allow the gate to open on its own. Inside was pitch blackness. Amaya swallowed the lump in her throat and grabbed some decorative candles, lighting three of them. The gothic sentiment was not lost on her as she felt like a classic character chasing after Nosferatu. She needed to duck down to enter the small frame but once she passed the opening the inside lair was huge in scope. As she attempted to look at the vastness with her candlelight, the door slammed shut behind her. She jumped as all the candles blew out instantly.

Amaya ran from The Majic Shoppe. She left the memory of her grandmother's body gutted open and red, the potions and charmed promises of the business, and the black door of wonder behind her. She huffed and puffed, breathing heavier with each stride. Everything that happened was hazy except the clear memory of the Butyanko. She thought back to the demon.

Its eyes.

Its black top hat.

The sigil that had burned demonically on the ground all around her as she had told it what she wanted.

It listened.

It had heard her request.

Amaya left her village behind her and took the last running bus out. She traveled as close as she could get to Bran Castle; home to the legendary Vlad "The Impaler" Tepes, Bran was one of the impervious fortresses on top of the Carpathian Mountains. Also, it was where her mother dove off after deciding the love of a daughter wasn't enough in this world. The young macabre dreamer knew she'd need to pace herself to make it up the 1500 steps that lead to the castle's gates.

The Butyanko said, "You will be visited tonight." That's all she needed to hear. She knew just where to be swept away from and had to get there.

When Amaya was 700 steps into the climb, she saw a wobbly intoxicated man from the village swaying and staggering down the cement stairs. She knew from past encounters he was no good; he was hateful, really. She clenched her fists, expecting the worst. He called to her immediately while swinging a bottle.

The drunkard preached loudly and slurred, "Look at you all bloody girl, I wanna tell you something… I am not a racist person; I believe that everyone should be treated equally, regardless of ethnicity or culture. But, having grown up around here where I have to face gross gypsies like you every single time I leave the house, always begging me for money. It becomes tiring and I've come to hate most of you. I wasn't always this way, I appreciate the gypsies who actually work and try to make a living, but they're a minority within a minority. Most gypsies just beg at the age of 25 so they can feed their 10 children. And it's not like the government hasn't tried to integrate you fuckers, ya know; they've built apartment buildings for you and tried to get them to work, but that's just how you are. Some want to just kill your kind; there is no possible way to integrate ya. And yeah, that is why I hate you people now. Okay?" Amaya had heard this before, from everyone. This was why she was over this life and over these people who judged her without knowing her. She would be better, soon. "And now you're calling yourselves 'Romani' because 'Gypsy' became a racial slur. You did that yourself, you know -Gypsy wouldn't be a racial slur if you hadn't made a name for yourselves as thieves, liars and criminals. That's who you are, even you girl. I've been Gypt'ed before on deals. Everybody has."

Amaya tried to ignore the comments as she continued her climb on towards his direction. He was looking at her as a caterpillar, but soon the world would see the emergence of the butterfly. She knew this to be true and had seen the door to prove it.

"Hey cunt, why do you people steal from old ladies and beat young children. Why do you cut down WHOLE forests, and even murder?" Amaya never murdered anyone, sacrifice was another story... "You trash don't want to work because if you have many children you receive welfare and the children will start asking for money or stealing on the streets. There, gypsies even send their wives and children as prostitutes..." He threw an empty bottle in her direction. It shattered on the steps between them. "Are you a prostitute girl? Hey whore; there are two reasons for the very short life span of gypsies." He laughed at his own thoughts. "You are all dirty; I can usually recognize a gypsy by smell faster than by appearance, and you know they become addicted to smoking very early at 11-12-13. I assure you that nobody forces you to neither smoke nor stay filthy; it's because you are trash. That's what you are."

The two stood a few steps apart. He looked at her with hate for everything he felt she stood for, gypsy history, Romani culture, but he didn't know her future. Most days she'd be likely to agree with him that she was gutter trash, but not tonight; she'd come too far. Amaya crooked her head to the side and let her hair fall from her face. She tightened her fist around her dagger that was still bloody from the earlier bludgeoning. She had offered the only person who ever cared for her for a better life, and this man had the audacity to provoke her while Dracula waited for her at Bran Castle. She shouted, "I was a Romani Gypsy and I hate that you call them 'cunts.' If you are going around calling them thieves and cunts, then I don't care. I'm better than that, and I have no intention of stealing from someone, shit we have a store in town."

"I've seen your shop. Dealing with the devil is also what corrupts. Using evil leads to becoming evil, Sorcerer. I'll tell your grandma that you're out here too late, git you in a heap of trouble."

"Well, you're right, sir. Evil does corrupt, I just made a deal with the Devil tonight to escape this life and people like you." She pulled out the blade. "All of this blood on me is the blood of my own grandmother, so imagine what I'll do to you, ignorant fuck."

The drunkard put his hands up in front of his face in mock fright of the chubby dark youth and knocked the tool from her hand easily. Amaya watched in skip and fly, descending the steps. The drunk then began to stagger down the side of the stairs in the direction of the knife, scrambling away from this girl that he was sure had lost her mind. Amaya Mizelli watched him get ten steps below her as she pondered the perplexities of life; her old grandmother passed away on a night that this piece of human waste was allowed to live, and he's spewing his hate and ignorance. It didn't add up. She started crying harder as she climbed higher and higher towards Bran Castle and her new life. The site for so much pain would be her rebirth.

Nobody ever listens to me, she thought to herself. Nobody hears her except Butyanko. He had listened and heard her request. She thought back to what she had cleverly told Butyanko when it had given her its full attention. She chose her words carefully as to not get it twisted in execution. She had said forcefully, "I want it to float down to me and suck of my blood." She said this for three reasons. Number one, she never referred to him as a person living or dead, so that she felt Butyanko could not manipulate that to her detriment. Number two, she clearly mentioned it floating to her, for she knew her lover flies. Number three, she wanted very much for the bite to awaken her to pleasures not yet tasted of the flesh and afterlife. She had been clever. Unlike the others, she had covered all her bases. She had done what all her ancestors had failed to do, including her silly mother.

The pathway at the top of the stairs led to a growth of vine growing up the side of the classical structure; she had navigated many times before. She did not stop in her quest until she was in the open air atop the highest section overlooking the trees and sleeping village below her. How little they were beneath her and her eventuality. She looked down at her clothes and the dried blood that caked the linens. She unbuttoned her dress letting it all fall, choosing the under garments over the dress but found them besmirched and stained as well. This was to be her husband, she mused, so she opted for her nakedness. There she stood, exposed, cool in the night air on her flesh; an average girl in the moonlight with nothing left for this world. She waited for him to take her far from this place. She waited, pushing her chucha up and stretched her neck forward, hoping to appear radiant and accepting in the moonlight. She anticipated his first sight of her. She knew there would be no second chance at this. It couldn't be anything but love, and she was sure of it. He would fall for her, they would be together for an eternity, and then... She felt a tiny sting and looked at her left side. A mosquito landed on her dark skin, finished up its meal and flew away. She paid it no mind at first, thinking back to Dracula's smile and features. Then she suddenly understood what had happened, and a wave of anxiety and panic flushed over her every naked pore. Hair rose and skin bumped with gooseflesh as she examined what had just happened.

"No!"

After everything that had occurred this night. Her own words and request used against her.

"No!"

What she had done to get here. She had turned her back on everything to be better, to be more than trash and she had finally seen that there is another side to this world, and she was granted entrance for a glimpse of it. Now all that was ripped away. For her to go back to what? To what? She was plain, just like her mother before her. No money, no real opportunity and now it was worse. She took a cigarette and lighter from her pile of clothes. She lit it and puffed out as she looked to the vastness of the night. She flicked the butt from her fingertips and into the night; she watched the light flicker and disappear into the widening abyss. She rose herself up on the top section of the highest ledge, wondering if this was the exact location her mother had stood.

"I am bengalia after all..."

Amaya fell hard and fast, twisting and spinning from the peak of the rubble just as her mother had done almost eighteen years before. Amaya hoped she looked as beautiful in her death as her grandmother had. She closed her eyes as she struck full force into the rocks below. Her face exploded on impact and pieces tore off in a multitude of directions, leaving primarily only the torso intact. Torrents of water ran around and through the newly formed spouts in her mangled corpse, innards lay mashed between slabs and pebbles, all signaling to the universe the eventual demise of the Mizelli family. The Butyanko had won.

In the still of the night a cloaked figure stepped from the darkness. An ancient being with long claws that divided the living from the dead in ways humans could never comprehend. He knelt and smelled the bloody clothes she left behind. He then looked over the ledge to the rocks and depth below the castle, pausing for a moment, eyeing up the formless, perverted and distorted being of nakedness so far below. His aged eyes made clear all the details of what was left of the female before finally accepting this and exploding into a mist of bats that scattered off into the forever night.

2
———

D'MON

Two guards walked down the long hallway, leading to the off-limits prisoner holding area. It was dark and damp all around them as they walked along in silence. At the end of the hall, the cell block leader waited for them. The shorter guard spoke up first, "We are here for the transfer of inmate XXX6660."

The leader of this particular prison wing sat back behind the glass in his one room office. He eyed the guards up intently and said, "That prisoner is awaiting transfer. We've been waiting a long time for this."

The holder looked in the direction of the cell and continued. "It's been difficult for me and my boys not to do the AC's job for him. Don't know why it took this long for justice, but we knew this day would come." The leader smiled, showing the one large jagged fang that hung from his reptile mouth. The guards nodded and hurried past as he buzzed them in thru the main gate.

They walked along in silence for a while longer, passing other holding cells. All signs that life existed in the rooms were hidden from a passerby, but the guards had heard rumors of the kinds of horrors that continued to grow in these holding cells. Creatures that were far too destructive to be seen by society. Most were considered top secret failures of Hell, and out of all of them none had caused as much noise and problems as the one they were on a quest to recover.

When the guards reached the door XXX6660, they stopped and took a deep breath. With a flash of fear on his face, the younger guard looked at the older one.

"You'll be fine," grumbled the more experienced guard. "He's chained up and you know that. Don't be stupid."

While the frightened green skinned guard looked on, the more experienced shorter browner skinned one opened the panel on the side of the cell so he could he could talk through it, and he began standard transfer procedure. "Inmate number triple x, triple six, zero, Damien-ki Zakire Monteloflobe, you have been requested above ground by the High Council of the Under World. The current acting AC has shown great leniency and mercy in offering you an opportunity to avoid your current imprisonment and eventual sentence of eternal misery in the bottomless pit. You are very lucky, Damien-ki. Prepare yourself for transfer."

A voice rose from deep in the holding cell. It spoke with purpose and did not stutter. "I do not answer to that name any longer. I am D'mon."

The guards looked at each other in shock and amazement.

The smaller guard hit the iron bars with his billy club and shouted, "That name is forbidden! It is only to be spoken of by the High Council. Do you understand?"

"It is who I am."

"That person does not exist, *Damien-ki*. He never did. Prepare yourself now for transfer!" With those words, the older, shorter guard motioned for the younger, taller, more lanky guard to crank the lever pulling at the chains running along the side of the wall. He turned and turned the circular crank, which in turn pulled thick chains taut that led to the cell. Once the inmate had been stretched out, the guards entered the cell and bore witness to this legendary traitor in shackles. The thick chains hung him up by his arms. With his arms over his head, his powerfully fastened nude body could be clearly made out by the guards.

He appeared how he'd been depicted in writings and spoken about amongst hushed circles. The light from the doorway shone on his reddish tinted flesh. It was a sign of his birth into the demon community, and overall, his chiseled features and muscular physique made him look more like a model. He had thick lips and dreadlocks that hung from his horned head, signaling that he was from the Jamaican portal of Hell. Hairy muscular legs led to what had been rumored to be hooves, but they instead were his clawed feet which stomped angrily at the ground.

The guards walked close to the prisoner standing directly beside him.

As D'mon's eyes adjusted to the light, he saw his guards clearer. The smaller guard was leathery and had various moles all over him. He looked much like a human crossed with a toad. His yellow eyes showed no signs of kindness or understanding, only ages and ages of enjoying the torment of others. D'mon was familiar with that look, he'd had it once himself.

The younger guard was taller, thinner, and looked as though he could play on Hell's own basketball team (if such a thing existed). His face and hands were a light green, but with a clearer complexion. His eyes had a bright orange glow to them. D'mon immediately sensed there was far less evil in him. He had not yet completely turned.

He thought they looked like a frogman and a toad man. *How interesting*. He looked at the guards and spoke, "They sent two imps to pull me from this prison? I shall call you Toad and Frog. Where's Mical?"

"That's enough out of you," Toad exploded. He took his thick side stick with the glowing red tip and jammed it into D'mon's side. D'mon kicked and screamed as the hellfire electricity ran thru his body.

Frog, the younger imp watched, as D'mon's head fell back in submission. "See that, kid?" Toad said. "That's how you keep these pieces of garbage in line."

The two guards adjusted the chains which held the demon tightly from his shackled claw-feet all the way to his shackled hands and led him through the hallways, past the various guards and cell holders who always hollered and shouted their approval.

"Kill the bastard!"

"Make him suffer!"

Everyone they passed was philosophically against everything that D'mon had once stood for.

Once they made it to the elevator, the doors closed, and the older imp selected the codes to their destination. They stood in silence, waiting. It was a lengthy trip with both imps uncomfortably shifting in the tight quarters with this abomination. It was intimidating even in shackles; the whole ride in the elevator Frog hoped the chains would hold. When the doors opened again, a familiar sight greeted D'mon. He anticipated meeting the High Council of the Underworld. Mentally and physically strong as he appeared, deep inside his stomach twisted in a knot.

The guards led him across the thick metal cliff that hung suspended in air, leading to the center where the council waited. All sides of the metal cliff were lined with a severe drop. They were far above the licks, and fiery torment that lost human souls knew to be eternal damnation. Below him stood the reward that many a human evil doer could expect after their lives have ended on the surface. Standing at their positions in rows stacked high along the walls of the cave, the leaders from all corners of the Underworld watched. Every providence and corner of Hell was represented. The current reigning AC stood at a large black elegant podium, and addressed his people, if you could call them that. The AC kept his back to D'mon, but he recognized the robe.

The guards walked the demon to the center and halted in front of their leader. D'mon kept his eyes down; he did not want to see what creature of damnation would be responsible for his future. There was a brief moment of hushed silence before it spoke, and then came the familiar voice, "Do you think these leaders came to see the great Damien-ki Zakire Monteloflobe, today?"

The demon prisoner turned his head to see his worst enemy as it rose in the air. Of course, they promoted Ray Ma Ching. He had once gotten banished; that lying piece of shit con-artist Ray Ma Ching was one of the top salespeople Hell had to offer. Ray wasn't the best, though; D'mon knew who the best was. He knew who was truly responsible for dooming more human fates than anyone. He watched as Ray's fat little Asian demon body hung in the air. Showing off. *It's all just tricks,* D'mon thought, *tricks and gifts bestowed on the AC by He Who Reigns.* He'd seen this all before; if he was to be tormented, he didn't need the special effects. He wasn't impressed.

As he hovered in air shooting bolts of hellfire electricity, Ray's eyes made contact with D'mon for the first time. His face was a cluster of pulsing veins that ran along his cheeks and his forehead. His skin had grown even more doughy since D'mon had seen him last, and when he spoke it reminded D'mon of everything wrong with this place. He looked away to his sides to see the two guards who stood with hellfire electric batons ready.

"I asked you a question, do you think these leaders came to see you today?" The AC swung back and forth in the air and continued, "Do you think they came here to commend your treachery, your lies, your turning your back on your people? No, that's not it. For what you have done, the crimes you've committed against our society, you deserve to be torn apart by a thousand ratigans!" He rolled the R for emphasis, making it sound much more like rrrrrrrrrratigans. The council reacted loudly; ratigans were feared in Hell, even amongst these strong leaders. No one fucked with a ratigan. That surely was a punishment befitting such a traitor, and everyone approved.

Ray Ma Ching lowered himself to D'mon's level and got in the subdued Demon's face. He said, "These great and powerful leaders have gathered to see the great hero D'mon *on his knees!*" He shot D'mon's body with multiple bolts from the blackness of his flowing robe. The pain that hit D'mon was excruciating; he bucked and twisted against the chains. Toad smirked and let him fall forward onto his face. From his new position, D'mon saw thru the many holes on the metal walkway, and he could make out the bubbling redness flowing over itself in excitement far below. It flowed like lava in a volcano or a mass of fat worms. He could make out the specs that were mixed in the redness, like ants on a pile of sugar. He knew what they were. Human souls were being tortured, raped, and molested until the end of days. Another lifetime ago, a large portion of these souls had been personally brought to hell by D'mon. Back then he felt differently; he was proud of filling the place up. He felt differently about what a human soul was, and he didn't consider it was even worth a damn.

Knowing what D'mon knew now about these humans, he couldn't help but feel sorry for this kind of fate. *What kinds of things could these people have done on the surface that would bring them this as a punishment?* Impulse decisions usually landed humans into this fate, and humans regretted it later, when it was too late.

D'mon felt regret for his involvement in this cycle. Sadly, it would continue on with or without his involvement in it. He could clearly see Ray was the next in charge to be worshipped as The Antichrist. If the end of days been called upon, this stupid asshole in a robe would be in charge to lead Hell toward its attack and conquer Earth along with whatever other planets had intelligent life in the cosmos. D'mon knew that some of the High Council represented parts of the universe; although they had life energy or breath of life, they did not have the power of a human soul.

Hellfire energy tore through him a second time, causing a scream to escape from D'mon and brought his attention back. Ray stood proudly behind him and continued, "Damein-ki, you were once one of the greatest soul traders of all time. You brought more souls into Hell than any anyone else. You were powerful, respected, and could have had it all. But you threw it away to live on the surface with the humans. You became a fugitive, an outlaw. You became *D'mon*."

Disruptions arose from the council as they rumbled at his blasphemy.

"How pathetic to think that at one time you were almost considered Antichrist material; you!" Ray Ma Ching laughed at the notion and looked on at D'mon's present state. Even as he lay in pain and chains, D'mon felt pity for Ray and the whole industry; being an AC meant so much to Ray, and that was pathetic.

When D'mon was offered the role of AC, he turned it down on multiple occasions; he knew that the by the day-to-day grind of Hell's admission sales job was bad enough without needing to be in charge of motivating and leading its team. It was a dead-end position, and D'mon regretted nothing in leaving this wretched place. Ray eyed this traitor of Hell before continuing, "Lucifer, in his grand mercy, has agreed to offer you a chance to redeem yourself to this council. All you need to do is accomplish what you used to do on a regular basis. You just need to do your job."

D'mon looked up from the metal mesh. *No.*

"There is a soul that burns brightly on the surface."

No, please.

"We have not seen a soul as powerful in centuries."

Please, God no.

"Lucifer has chosen you to claim it for us."

Fighting back anger, frustration, and even surprising to himself-tears, D'mon crawled to a sitting position and spoke, "Why me?"

"Because you are a soul trader, a demon. You tried to run from your lot in life once Damein-ki, but it's time you owned up to what you are. Do not question what our Dark Lord has laid out for you. You are being given the opportunity of your life spared in exchange for this human soul. Just do your job and don't fuck it up. We all know how easily manipulated these humans are. Study up on your sales material and give it what it wants. The buzzwords and the catch phrases, these people are all the same; offer it a car, or a house, or the love of its favorite mate. Who cares? Just bring its soul back to us and you will be released and rewarded. Proving your usefulness, you will work for me; but if you fail, then you will be cast immediately into the bottomless pit with no more vacations in that prison. Along your way to the pit, you may be meeting various ratigans on the way down. Pass or fail, either way this council will be pleased."

From his knees, D'mon scanned the council of the underworld and saw that it still looked much the same as he'd remembered, various fucktards that resembled insects and creatures he had seen from the surface. There were monsters resembling large snakes, scorpions, spiders, hundred-legged worms, and other unfriendly evilness that's presence would make a human squirm. If some human imagines it or fears it, it comes to pass, somehow living and breathing here; Lucifer has seen to that. These minions of Hell all chattered their teeth and stomped their feet loudly, awaiting his answer. Below them all the lifeblood of Hell bubbled up and continued to roll over itself in anticipation. He knew Lucifer waited.

It wasn't much of a choice.

D'mon nodded his head.

Ray smiled.

3

IN SEARCH OF THE CHUPACABRE

arky Mark Acosta walked down the steps of the unassuming white building in the heart of Hollywood, CA. He was aware that he looked like a stereotypical Hispanic gang member. He had a bandanna on his head, and a long sleeve button up flannel shirt that was only buttoned at his neck, letting the sides fall open as he walked. His jeans were ripped and dirty. He stopped at a newsstand to pick up a copy of the *Los Angeles Times*. He walked across the street, thru the busy traffic, and made his way to the white van that said, "MODERN IRRIGATION AND LAWN CARE" on it. He opened the driver's side door and tossed the newspaper on the passenger seat. Once he'd closed the door, his tough exterior cracked a bit. He turned the radio up to try to take his mind off another failed audition. As the Mariachi music got louder, he openly wept; his tears fell on his hands. All his training in theater and performance, and yet he was had not been taken seriously.

With his right hand, he opened the glove compartment and withdrew one of his many piled up Hollywood headshots. He studied the black-and-white photo of himself with his name at the bottom; he was looking so eager to be the next big thing in Hollywood. *Why did it have to be so difficult?* He turned the paper over in his hands to look at his standard entertainment resume on the other side. It was broken into its three columns about the small roles and webisodes he'd been in since moving to Los Angeles. He tore the headshot and resume in half, then crumpled it into a ball and threw it down.

A familiar tune rang out. He picked up his cell phone to see who it was. It was his day-job boss, and he took the call begrudgingly.

"So, how'd it go?" asked the older Latino gentleman on the other side of the call.

"Not so good, Alex, I went through all kinds of hell getting there, dealing with parking and the casting company, and then they said that I'm not Hispanic enough! Never mind that my entire family is from Mexico. These Hollywood people are stupid."

"Yeah. Well, fame doesn't just happen overnight Marky. You gotta put years in. You should know that. You should just give that shit up and focus on your trade. You ain't so bad at that."

Marky Mark Acosta wasn't paying attention as he read the cover of the latest edition of the newspaper. Well,Something fantastical had grabbed his attention.

"Hey if you hurry, you can get my van back to the shop tonight."

"No, that's not necessary; you know I'm good for it. Think I'll hold on to it a while longer." He laughed and then added, "I got an idea that can change everything."

"Goddamn it, Marky! You can't just run off and steal the company van. You wanna get fired or thrown in jail? Goddamn it! I keep trying to help you, and all you do is fu..."

After Mark clicked off his cell phone, he sat back in his seat and looked out the window. He started up the van and drove through the heart of Hollywood. Alex called him back, and he let it go straight to voicemail, all three times. On both sides of the road, Mark saw many faces of wannabes walking around Hollywood. He knew there were even more that arrived every day. He flipped his radio over from the Mexican Ranchero music that had been playing to the AM news stations, and they all were giving their thoughts on the latest news. That's how he knew he was on the right path; everything had changed, and he was eager to become a part of this new world.

Early morning word of the mysterious killings in Maryland had spread everywhere in the media, just as the police chief at the scene had said. Local news crews were on the scene before the authorities were notified, and witnesses had social media in a tizzy over it. It had leaked fast. Perhaps too fast. As shocking as the brutal murders were, it was the sensational parts of it that the media clung to tightly. There were the reanimated corpses, flying saucers, and sentient talking gelatinous goo invaders. First, there was the discovery that some kind of breed of vampire or undead regeneration did in fact exist. No joke, no James Randi worthy skepticisms, no tricks or magic, it was real science, and it was for all to see. It was fully exposed too fast for the government to "Area 51" the whole event.

The huge news rocked the world.

The footage was taken at the scene by news crews and media personelle, so this wasn't something anyone could sweep under the rug. It attracted all kinds of attention from people worldwide, and reports started coming in about what else could be true. Speculations were made about everything from ghosts, to Bigfoot, to sea serpents, haunted dolls, even more classic vampires, and of course even monsters under your bed. Every talking head on television had a point to make about what was real and what evidence had never been a hoax.

At the center of the media whirl, was a young opportunistic Bud Parker, who according to him, not only survived a vampire attack by the first ever discovered monsters, but had single-handedly killed it. Talk of the sensational, chiseled jawed Bud Parker, Vampire Hunter, was everywhere. In one interview, he had encouraged all vampires to come see him; that he had something for them. Bud was the new self-appointed hero, and Marky couldn't stand it. Talk of his own reality show swirled as his likeness was put on t-shirts and merchandise over-night.

Marky watched how this dude became the new sensation. He listened intently to all the details about how this guy had discovered a modern-day vampire and lived to tell the story, even though his own family didn't. The whole situation brought up more questions than answers with some people, and he was at the center of it all.

Hmmm, this is crazy, he thought to himself.

As he came up on a red light, he reached over to the passenger's seat and turned his newspaper over to look at the cover again. There he was, "BUD SURVIVES REAL VAMPIRE ATTACK." There was a picture of him with his arms crossed and his hair falling down around his superhero face. He wasn't smiling. He had a serious and almost intimidating look to it. That somehow amused Mark. The picture had been taken in a cemetery, and his crossed arms seemed to say, "Bring it on, fucker."

The light turned green, and as Marky started driving again towards his destination, he imagined that celebrity having all kinds of books written about his adventures. He was going to be featured on the news and probably was being offered his own goddamn reality show. *They'll probably even make a movie outa this.* Marky had struggled for years to make it in entertainment as an actor, but he rarely made it past a callback; and here Bud is, just slipping right into the limelight. Well, he'd had enough.

Here was another example of how messed up the industry was. Marky knew that this vampire thing - while uncommon in America - wasn't as big news to his family in Mexico. He thought back to his childhood and all the things he'd heard about. There were a few things he'd seen, but never fully understood. He'd decided that if finding proof of vampires was what America needed to make him a star, he knew just where to go.

Jose Acosta had been telling the people in his small Mexican town for years about the vampires near his farm, but nobody would listen. Late at night, the *goat suckers* would attack his livestock and carry away whatever pleased them. It had pissed him off for as long as he could remember; in the later years of his life, he'd gotten used to staying in at daybreak. He tried not to let a few missing animals get to him. The alcohol helped. He'd heard stories of small children being carried away by the evil dogs, but he hadn't experienced any of that. Besides, after his wife left him and took the kids, it was just the goats and livestock they mainly came for. On particularly depressing nights, when his brain was on fire with memories of his wasted life, he wished they'd come for him too.

This was one of those nights. Jose sat at his favorite pub and drank tequila at his usual black table in the back. The number of bottles on the surrounding table grew larger and larger as the night wore on. Jose was an overweight Hispanic man with sad eyes and hairy arms. He motioned with his hand at the girl to bring him more. She was a young petite thing, and he had enjoyed watching her tiny body bring him the alcohol. This time she brought a bucket with ice filled with many bottles of beer.

"I thought this'd be faster for you," she said. "Save me some trips."

Jose smiled at her through glazed over eyes, and with all the charm of a garden slug said, "Well look at you. You're the booze cooze, ain't cha?"

Jose hoped that it had come out as smooth as he'd intended it to. Maybe they would live happily ever after, or at least get their rocks off after the bar closed up. By the look on her face, it hadn't gone over quite as well.

He dropped some pesos on the table and looked away. *Well, who needs ya anyway whore?* When he looked back, she'd moved on and was talking with a table of younger men. Jose looked into his bottle and cursed his life. He thought she was probably flirting with them. One of the men at the table hollered over at Jose, something he barely understood. He wanted to ignore them, but one word made him take notice: *Chupacabra.* Jose couldn't help himself. He stood up.

"Yeah, I see it. I see it every other week. It's real and smelly and it's real..."

He trailed off in a drunken slur as the boys laughed at him.

One of them yelled back at Jose, "You sure it's not a mirror you're coming across there Pedro? You're pretty damn smelly yourself." They all had a laugh at Jose the town drunk - Jose the town idiot.

A while later the commotion died down. They had gone, and Jose sat alone with one bottle left in his bucket. He mumbled to himself, "I know what I seen."

After a few hours of steady driving through the border, Marky Mark thought better than to go straight to the farm. Instead, he pulled the white work van up to the local pub. He opened the door, jumped out, and ran up the stairs to the screen door entrance. It'd been a few years since he'd seen this corner of the world, but he knew all the stories. This man he was about to visit had basically replaced his family with alcohol. It seemed like a bad choice to Marky. Most of what Jose talked about these days was his farm falling apart, drinking, and the *goatsuckers*.

Marky entered the dingy bar and noticed it was almost empty. There were only a few scattered drinkers in the place, a few women minding the bar, and a lonely filthy drunk taking up space in the back. Marky walked to the bartender and asked, "How many has he had tonight?"

"What do you think," came the bartender's reply. "If you know him, you should just get him the hell outta here. Kind of pathetic, you know, bad for business?" Marky nodded and walked to the back. Jose was slumped over on the table.

Marky Mark grabbed him around the waist and said, "Let's get you out of here."

"Marky" he slurred. "Marky, I seen 'em, but nobody believes me."

Mark walked him slowly to the door. "I believe you Uncle Jose. I believe you."

Then Mark noticed the line of dampness that lead down his uncle's pants to a pool growing on the floor. His uncle had just pissed his pants.

Only after Jose was safely in the passenger's side of the white van with that newspaper laid out on the seat for his stanky urine-soaked ass, Mark drove off towards the Mexican farmhouse. He looked over at this sorry excuse for a human being, who looked every bit the piece of shit his family had told him he was. Still, he felt bad for him. He wondered how a man could let himself go like this.

They pulled off the main street toward the house. The dirt road kicked up a dirt cloud all around that coated the van. *The house, what a funny thought.* Mark hadn't been anywhere near this area in a long time, but he still remembered what it was like when all was well between the families. There used to be sunny days, water fights, and laughing. There was a lot of laughter. There were forests of trees on all sides of the road leading to the house, giving it a very isolated feeling. Marky thought that if everything was true about this place, then why in the hell would his uncle choose to stay here. Why would any sane person live where vampire dogs came at night to snack on the livestock, chickens, and goats? Wouldn't it only be a matter of time until they started moving up the food chain? It just didn't make any sense. Then Mark turned to look at his smelly drunk passenger that sat slurring in his sleep and realized common sense wasn't his uncle's strong point.

The white van pulled up to the end of the driveway of the looming dark casa. As he helped Jose out of the truck and in the direction towards the dwelling, he felt a strong gust of wind whip by. He looked at a wooden duck that was positioned in the yard. Normally this duck's arms would swing in circles in a breeze, but its arms stayed just as they were.

Mark realized it wasn't the wind that had blown past, but something else. He looked up at the ominous building which sat beneath the darkened sky. He stood still and watched everything for any signs of something that shouldn't be there.

The farm animals started acting up. It was as though they knew that something wasn't right and that indeed the world was changing all around. Marky's hair on the back of his neck stood up. He held his breath. Jose mumbled something as a line of drool ran out of his mouth. He spat something into the grass yard. Mark took his hands off this gross old man and watched him crumple into the grass like a slinky.

Marky motioned with his hands for the old fool to stay quiet.

Jose looked at him and mumbled something again, only this time laughed, and then repeated what he had said, only this time louder.

"We're sooo fucked."

Marky looked up from the drunk and saw *them* standing there; this was the first time he'd seen them since he was nine years old. He hadn't been hallucinating or making it up; they'd been just as real as they were now. Four of them stood maybe a hundred yards away. They were hairless demonic muscular perversions of dogs standing on all fours, and they had glowing red eyes. Their mouths harbored defined fangs that they showed off in snarls. A low growl came from the two that were closest to the men. The vampire-dogs dared him to move.

This was what Marky wanted to find, but instead it found him. He just hadn't expected it so damn soon. If he could slay one that would be his proof that Bud wasn't the only Vampire Hunter out there with balls of steel. He had found them relatively easy, almost too easy; and now he knew that he needed to document this. *My iPhone! Dammit!* Marky Mark Acosta cursed his having left it in the van. He left Jose and slowly took a step backward toward the door. He looked through the driver's side window and saw it lying on the space between the two front seats. The Chupacabra moved closer to him with open, salivating jaws.

As quickly as he could, Marky rushed to the van and stood by the driver's side door with his hands on the handle. One of the unholy dogs was right behind him and charged Mark with its open mouth, eager to taste his flesh. He turned the handle of the door and opened it hard; this surprised the creature and hit it hard in the face. Mark heard the thud against the door and watched it bounce back on the grass with a whimper. The other three hell hounds gathered around the open door and inspected the fallen member of their pack. Mark slid into the van and tried to close the door behind him, but the dogs were already coming in after him.

They were vicious in their attack with snapping jaws. He stomped at the hairless rat-like faces with his boots until he was finally able to close the door completely behind him. Only once he was safe and secure in the van did he remember that Jose was still there.

Looking through the window, Marky saw the dogs surrounding his overweight uncle. Marky knew this man had a zero chance of surviving. Jose attempted to stand and was staggering backward, almost out of Marky's view. He watched as his pathetic uncle took a swing at one; the Chupacabra attacked him at once. One tore into his leg while another lunged at his middle, and then they disappeared off into the darkness near the chicken coop.

The wannabe celebrity sat in the van, imagining the horrible attack. He looked for a weapon to take with him, but only found the iPhone. He picked it up, turning it over in his hand to discover the flashlight feature. Remembering that these things aren't seen during the day, Mark hoped the light would be good enough to scare them off.

He held it tightly, hit the RECORD button and the flashlight feature at the same time, and spun around to face the incoming threat.

The light from the camera phone hit the area near the van; strangely, there was nothing to see but the grass and nothing to hear but the quiet of the night. Marky was on edge as he walked hurriedly around, pointing the camera in different directions. Looking through the lens of the camera phone, he looked again at the chicken coop, then at the farm animals. The farm animals had settled down, as if they no longer feared that at any moment they could be next.

Marky eyed Jose's house and ran up onto the porch. He first opened the screen door, then the larger door, all the while fearing that any moment he could be attacked from behind. He did make it in. Upon entering the home, Hosehead, Jose's large white Siberian husky greeted him at the door.

"Not now," Marky said as he patted the dog's head and rushed past him to find a real weapon. He took the old family rifle from its rack above the fireplace, checked it for bullets, and stood in the living room trying to muster the courage to go back out there. *My Uncle Jose might already be dead.*

He thought about all the things he had left to accomplish in his life. He was going to be a big movie star; Marky didn't want to risk this attack. He looked at himself in the mirror. If his face got marked in any way that would cut his marketability considerably in the entertainment world. Was the risk worth the reward? He looked at Hosehead in the corner, happily chewing on a magazine he had stolen from that day's mail. That damn dog didn't seem the least bit troubled; he was completely oblivious to the devastation outside. Briefly, Marky envied him. He reached for the dog and attempted to take the magazine from his mouth. After a slight tug, Hosehead let it go; there on the cover of the magazine was America's *new hero,* Bud Parker.

Marky Mark Acosta looked at the magazine in disgust and exclaimed, "Motherfucker!"

Feeling he had no choice, he dropped it back to Hosehead, and rushed back outside in search of Jose and his future.

Armed with only his iPhone, loaded rifle, and a ballsy sense of pride, Marky took a few steps off the porch and aimed his weapon to the heavens. The warning shot made his heart beat even faster in his chest. He hoped it scared the creatures as much as it had frightened himself. He took more steps toward the area he'd last seen the pack, shaking with each step. Perspiration ran down his face, and eventually he made it over the coop.

Jose was just past the chicken holding area. He was face down in the mud of the farm animal's stall. His clothes were ripped and torn, and all four *goatsuckers* appeared to be *human-suckers* as they had their mouths attached to Jose's body. They were sucking at his flesh while pulling back with their bodies. His flesh was stretched out at all four suction areas where the mouths were connected. Their eyes were closed in ecstasy over tonight's big meal. Mark heard the slurping, sucking sounds as he watched them gulping with their long necks. It reminded him of seeing a snake eating a group of small eggs.

He walked up to their meal and took aim at one of the dogs. He pulled off the shot and recoiled from the blast. It hit the creature right in its midsection. Blood and bits blew all over Jose and his fellow tormenters. It flew back and lay dead in the farm slop. The others immediately let go of Jose, and they took an offensive position, growling and snapping their jaws in Marky's direction. He didn't know if he could kill all three, but he would try.

position,He fired repeatedly at the others, but they moved fast after letting go of Jose. Then the three of them disappeared into the vastness of the farm. As they went away, Marky heard their cries. It was a mixture between a howl and a whine.

Not knowing if they were really gone, he walked slowly to Jose. He was aware that at any moment they could be back. He imaged them slipping around to the other side of the coop to surprise him, or perhaps coming back with more monster friends to assist them in their big game hunt.

His uncle was beyond dead. Some parts of him were practically hamburger from the mauling. He was a pile of torn ligaments and ripped muscles, and his ribs showed through. After going through the motions a few times in practice to get in "character," Marky turned on the live streaming function and began to cry on camera about losing his sweet uncle to the vampires. He kept note that the live viewers were increasing. He was sure to get all the gruesome footage and cry through it all. When he felt that he had enough footage and views to spread the word to be viral, he turned off both the camera as well as his fake tears. He started to head back to the house carrying with him a body of one of the vampire dogs, and he wore a big knowing grin. *This is how it all begins for me.*

Mark laid the evidence on the kitchen table. He opened Jose's refrigerator and took out random lunch meat and ate it whole from the plastic wrap. Hosehead sat nearby, waiting. Mark took tap water from the faucet into his cupped hands; and after he drank a few gulps, he immediately regretted being in LA too long. He went to Jose's bedroom, crashed on his big dusty bed, and fell asleep almost as soon as his head hit the pillow. As Mark lay in the room filled with various clutter, porno magazines, and boxes, he dreamed of the fame and fortune lifestyle he deserved and that had always eluded him. Hosehead looked on from the hallway while pushing his empty water bowl with his nose.

Marky opened his eyes to the start of a great day. He rose out of bed refreshed and happy. His struggles were finally over; this other vampire hunter bastard was no more heroic than he. He went into the kitchen and made the finest eggs, ham, and toast breakfast that he had ever made. God, it was delicious and the whole time his uncle's dog didn't bother him. Hell, he hadn't even seen the thing which was fine by him. It wasn't until he was putting the dishes in the sink that he thought about taking some more pictures with the Chupacabra body, just in case.

That was when he had the biggest chill down his spine.

The fucking body!

Where is it? He was sure he'd left it on the table last night. When he looked under the tablecloth, he saw worms and various bugs under there. Even large insects ran from leftover food. He turned to look for Hosehead. When he checked his normal hiding spots, he didn't find him. Only white fur all over and clumps of flesh from the big dog were scattered around like it'd been skinned in the night. His flesh was matted with mud as though he'd been drug thru a sewer. It was all very strange.

"What the hell," Marky exclaimed in shock. He couldn't fathom how this could have happened. Mark remembered the body of the Chupacabra from last night; he had brought it here.

"Son of a bitch," Marky couldn't believe this. After checking on his Facebook account and playing back the footage, he saw that the video was still intact. At first, he was relieved, thinking this would be his ticket. But after reading some comments, he saw that some people accused him of faking it all, the whole thing. This could come off like a Bigfoot sighting or an alien abduction, that's not what Mark needed. He sat down on a chair in the living room and looked over at the clumps of Hosehead. He was beyond frustrated, he needed answers to what was going on, and what he should do. Damn it, it was hard enough to get a body the first time. He leaned back in the chair and heard whispers. Tiny feet moving back and forth above him; he dared not look up, fearing this was all in his head, but eventually he had to look up.

When he tilted his head back, he couldn't fathom what he saw; it made no intelligent, realistic sense. All at once a massive swarm of insects that had gathered above him dropped down all over Mark in one swift motion. Centipedes, cockroaches, spiders, and others covered his shoulders and invaded his orifices. His ears and eyes bled as things twitched, squirmed, and burrowed into him; he gagged on the invaders that came from all angles. His ears filled with screamed torment, and the smell was horrendous. He twisted and threw his body around in a giant spasm in order to free himself, but nothing worked after much thrashing about. Marky Mark Acosta laid completely still on the stained living room carpet; the new great vampire hunter lay dead.

Marky opened his eyes and gained consciousness in a vast white space. At first, he freaked out with his hands brushing his body, but he found no bugs on him. He was clean and safe. He could make nothing out of anything and wasn't sure if he was alive, dead, or something in between.

He seemed to be suspended in this realm all alone. How long had he been here?

All at once, he knew that his arms were stuck, caught on a never-ending silver web. It was a giant spider's web that seemed to go for eternity in all directions. Marky was caught in the middle of it. He twisted and fought the sticky metal, but a part of him knew instinctively that he'd always been there; he was forever caught on this web.

A demonically inspired perversion of an insect awoke with Mark's thrashing about. It crept its way along the stitching; it appeared injured from a past incident, because it was dragging its mangled and crushed parts along, leaving a trail of blood or some juice behind it. It came to rest near Marky. It was as large as him and looked directly at him. Its large Disney'esq eyes blinked multiple times and stared. Mark's brain was instantly on fire.

"I believe your people call me El Cacuay."

Marky thought about the comment *my people* huh, *racist fucking spider,* but he wasn't going to say anything. He felt very vulnerable and beyond confused as he thought about how it had said El Cacuay. He sincerely worried about his sanity as he mouthed the words, "The Boogie Man?"

"Boogie-person really," it immediately snapped. With each word, the insect showed no signs of where the words were coming from. It just had giant blink-blink eyes. Marky felt it was as if the words were coming from inside his own head directly. This thing spoke by burning his brain with thoughts. He'd never taken drugs, but he wondered if this was like a bad trip.

"This is beyond a bad trip, son." It responded as it tilted its head to the side forever staring, "Before I'm done, you'll wish this was all a drug."

Realizing nothing was sacred, not even his thoughts, Marky screamed into the whitened abyss; he momentarily lost his mind in a fit of tossing and flipping about, still caught in this void, almost blacking out. The insect lurched forward, showing its underside, exposing something that resembled a mouth. It adjusted itself and drove its mandibles deep into his head, crunching on Mark's head like a peanut. Marky was sure he was dead; he felt it pull his brain out of his skull and wrench it free from his spinal cord.

There was blood that flung free and fell in great amounts deep below into the abyss. It seemed like it fell forever. *Where am I?*

Mark waited for the sweet promise of death, but it didn't come.

"Oh, you're not going anywhere. There'll be no relief. You are mine forever. You are mortally dead. Your soul has been released from its meat casing to wherever that goes. It's not my prerogative, but your breath of life, mmm, that's all for me, now."

Marky's brain was separated from his body, and he was tangled in the webbing.

"I can tear into you a million glorious ways, eating your ribcage, raping your urethra, separating your fingernails and bones, and you will never be saved by simply passing away. It won't happen. You are all mine! Breathe of life can exist here forever." It licked its mouth with a tongue darting out of a cavernous hole in its head.

"So, tell me my meat puppet, why would you come after us and anger my pets calling for *my* attention? Why do such a stupid thing?"

The incarnation of all things evil asked this of Marky's ripped out blood dripping brain; his body swung attached to the web.

"Why!" it demanded.

"Everyone knows about you now. It's because of Bud Parker; he told everyone!"

"BUD PARKER?"

"Yeah, yeah- he ah has proof of the supernatural in the world. That this all exists; more will come looking for you."

"Meat, if you are only saying this to protect your hide…"

"No," Mark insisted, as he could see a way out of this torment, whatever this place was. "No, I'll take you to him. Take him instead, torture that fucker."

While it contemplated, Marky felt the silence last forever. He wondered how long he had already been here. How long had his broken body hung on a web floating in white space? Just as he couldn't take this any longer the master moved forward and dislodged the brain from the webbing. Using one of its mighty legs, the skittering partially smashed bug raised his brain high over the drop to nothingness.

"Very well then, Marky my new meat puppet, you will take me to him, and I will visit with him as I have with you."

The creature dropped the brain; Marky's eyes on the empty shell of a head watched it fall fast. Consciousnesses spun around and around as part of him fell faster and faster until his dead eyes could no longer see anything at all.

Marky awoke in a panic, laying on the carpet in his Uncle's living room. He saw a few remaining insects and creepy crawlies around reminding him that it was real, and now he was to bring El Cacuay to Bud Parker. He stopped long enough to inspect his newly dead physical body in the mirror thinking only for a moment that he may be a bigger star as a zombie, but as soon as he considered it a flash in the mirror showed him an angry giant bug eyeing him from another world. "Don't fail me puppet," he heard in his brain.

Grabbing a few of his things, he ran to the van, and he drove off as fast as he could towards Maryland. And the new celebrity hero. *Finally, a role I can play effectively. Can't have the hero without a villain,* Marky thought to himself. *Well buckle up Hero, because here comes the goddamn Villain.*

4

CARGO

I'm Larry Urbas, and what I'm going to say doesn't make much sense. I'm currently quite fucked. I know that. I'm just hoping that maybe you can help me. See, I don't belong here, nobody does. This is insane. But the money was too good for me to ask any questions. I never should have looked in the back. He told me not to look—what I saw—it wasn't right—it wasn't right. Oh, but I'm getting ahead of myself here. As I said I'm Larry Urbas, and I hope you can help me.

I've been a truck driver for as long as I can remember. I got Lucy Jane Parnell pregnant in the 11th grade with our first son. In my years as a king of the open road, I've dealt with all the standard bullshit from homo boys at rest stops to white line fever, raging slabs, and more. I felt there was nothing I couldn't deal with.

That's why when I took the meeting with my new employer, I took the job without any questions. There'd never been a problem I couldn't deal with. My own will always being stronger than that of an asshole, or a surprise I'd run into on the road. I'm sure some of you men get what I'm saying here, swig of beer for the workin' man! Am I right? You're goddamn right I am. Sure, there were signs and red flags, and maybe, if I'd had more schooling, I'd have seen it coming. But, I'm a tad bit hardheaded and that's just how I've always been wired. Besides, it's hard to pay bills with hugs, kisses, and good intentions.

Sometimes you just need a risk to get your blood pumping.

For me that risk came from this fat, little, Hawaiian shirt wearing, S.O.B. that said he had a job for me to run some cargo out to Erie, Pennsylvania. Truth told, I was just pleased to see that a response to the ad I put up at the laundromat lead to real cash.

He wanted me to transport a black load or dark load. As he eloquently put it, a don't touch, don't look and we won't have to have problems load.

His beady little eyes stared holes into me, and he stressed how important this was to my future. Before that meeting, I'd only ever heard of this Hawaiian shirt fella before in passing whispers from other drivers at job sites. Tough men relayed that his mystery jobs paid well, and long ago, I'd decided that having never met him suited me just fine. Still, sitting across from him, my mind wondered what this was really about.

The whole thing had a mafia/mob feel about it, and it's not something I wanted to be associated with long term. It's hard to raise your family behind bars. Besides, I've seen too many guys end up in the slammer for something even more innocent than this. Who knows what I was being asked to run? It could have been guns, drugs, or dead bodies! Still, there was that thrill. The risk that anything could happen once I onetimewas on my way. The more we talked, the more I felt a stirring, a strong feeling that I wanted my story to share at biker bars. Dammit, he had me.

The boss man said his name was Tim Chizmar. He wanted this mystery load done—yesterday. I had ten hours to drive, and a deadline by a man who doesn't like to be kept waiting. I tried to tell myself this was a onetime thing and tried to look on the bright side. Hell, there was no snow or ice, and for October, I couldn't ask for better conditions. So there was that.

He said I'd be driving a standard Western Star Kenmore. I remember how he had eyed me up and added that it had 12 speeds and four reverse. He inquired if I could handle that. I was used to all this and told him so. He made a few more things very clear to me at that meeting, between sloppy bites of his barbeque wings and talking with his mouth full, shooting bits of meat in all directions—fucking fat slob. Even now, after everything that I've experienced, I still remember his words, "You don't look in the back of your truck. You don't question the cargo. You just deliver the goods, and when you get there, you don't look at who unloads it. Half money up front, the other half when you return, you do not look at what is in the back, ever. We understand each other?"

"We understand each other." I replied. Truth was, I just wanted to get it over with anyway. The gross little Hawaiian shirt man eyed me up and dabbed his mouth with a napkin before continuing on with all the details of my drive. As I looked at the purchase order, the guy who bought this drive from Chizmar was Eric Miller. Who the fuck is Eric *Miller*.

In a few days' time, I kissed the wife and kids' goodbye, left her some advance money from the job, picked up the truck from where the Hawaiian shirt man said to meet him, and I hit the road.

You're still with me, right? Good, because I'm not fucking around when I say I need you. There'll come a point where you'll see how my future depends on you. I'm desperate and scared and . . . and . . . I'll calm down, you need to understand. I'll explain.

So, I'm driving this truck, and it's okay at first. My Dwight Yoakam tunes were playing, and I felt like I was living the dream. Cars drove by with kids, fists raised, pumping their arms, and I tooted my horn; I do it, and they are pleased. Cars on the road made room to let me pass and flashed their high beams to make merging better. I was just thinking this would be a breeze when I noticed the shadows on the floor of the cab thickened. They collected and undulated like a living thing. They pooled and splashed around my feet, thick like oil. It crawled up my legs like millions of wriggling worms.

I tore my gaze away from the eerie darkness and blinked into the blinding light of the setting sun. All was normal outside my cab, but inside the slimy darkness crawled ever higher. I felt slimy, as if I had been dipped in sewer muck. Funny how my kids liked seeing things like Ninja Turtles skateboarding through sewer drains in cartoons, I'd seen that shit on their TVs and warned them that it isn't all fun; its turds, piss, and garbage down there. Fuckin hell, it's not a place to eat pizza those stupid heroes in a half shell, my ass. My rant made my kids smile, they'd laugh missing the solid points I was making, but anyway, I digress. My body was all of a sudden very gross and tainted by something not good, something wrong.

First, it appeared under the steering area by my feet, squishing and splashing about, and it was thick like oil. Instinctively I knew it wasn't a leak; I knew that this was madness. It smelled like an old bookshop, like very old pages. I remember how the smell brought back my childhood memories. I would wait for my grandma as she continually scoured the stacks of moldy old tomes. Her forever searching, and me forever bored. It was so weird. I shrugged it all off and kept driving.

Maybe this was a symptom of something. Of what, I didn't know. Maybe a weaker American would stop, but I was stronger than that. I'd told myself that I'd see a doctor about this once the load was delivered, and then I could afford to see a doctor.

Not long after that I heard knocking coming from the back. It had to be loud and powerful for me to hear that all the way in the cabin.

KNOCK KNOCK KNOCK KNOCK KNOCK

You have no idea how pissed off I was. I turned the radio up and it was as though the damn pounding turned up too. I was one cunt-hair away from pulling that truck off the road and into a tree just to stop it. Between the creepy crawly slimy feeling all over my body, the old book smell, and now this knocking …

KNOCK KNOCK KNOCK

I was going out of my mind. That's no bullshit. This is a straight shoot from me to you. Swatting my legs to stop the blackness, I began to panic. I'm not too strong to say that –shit what would you do? The smell, the books all around me, ink and pages, I couldn't take it. I just didn't have time for any hocus pocus bullshit. I pulled over to the side of a very busy highway. I got out and staggered a few steps. The pounding still rang out. I had no time for this, not on my job, not in my life.

KNOCK KNOCK KNOCK

A car sped past, lighting up the night for a moment as it blew by. I watched them drive past me, as if in another world.

KNOCK KNOCK KNOCK

I don't know how I got back to the hatch. It was like waking after sleepwalking.

My hands were on the handle. That's when the pounding inside stopped. There would be no more secrets. It knew where I was. I would break the rule, the one rule I was given.

Chizmar would be pissed, but I was eating the apple from the Tree of Knowledge. I needed to know. I lifted it. As the gate rose, I heard typewriter keys clicking. The WORDS. They washed over everything.

Such brightness all around.

The papers, the cuts.

Where's my arms, my legs, my face?

Where's my dick?

Where am I?

Now I'm just here. HERE. Not that I'd believe any of it anyway.

I'm another missing fuckhead. Why should you believe me?

Here's why, there's life and there's death. I know things in here. I miss my family. I miss life. I'm not a creation. I was there and now there's THIS. Whatever this is, I can SEE you. No, not like some author's creative fucking angle bullshit. I see you. I really do. I goddamn see you right now. You are holding me in your hands. I can see who you are and what you want. I see you. Stop reading RIGHT NOW. Go on, I dare you.

I thought so. See. I'm really talking to you right now. Please don't leave me in here. I'm scared! It's lonely in here…

You don't believe me. I can prove it to you. GODDAMN IT! Look at the facts.

Tim Chizmar and Eric Miller! I bet that bastard Chizmar took credit for this tale, huh?

Says he wrote it? Nah, he absorbed it. He knew I'd look; he knew it! Miller published it too huh? Look at the cover. Miller was the guy I was taking the load to!

I was the load. I was the cargo. They knew all along…

They used me. This book is full of crushed souls and broken dreams...
I will prove it to you... I have to...

Don't leave me in here. It's so cold…

5

———

FARKELBERRY FORREST CEMETERY

I n Farkelberry Forrest Cemetery, roughly six feet under the earth and dry rot, something unpleasant began to occur. A corpse, mostly rotted away and forgotten, lost to the ticking hands of time began to stir. The corpse, still with pieces of a fine suit holding its innards together, opened its dead eyes, looked straight ahead, and saw nothing but pure pitch-blackness everywhere. Fearing he was going blind, he began to panic before remembering where he was...

He grumbled; memories of another life came flooding back. He tasted death all around. He was in a coffin; ironically, he had picked it out himself. He'd always wondered what death tasted like, and now he knew. The taste of death reminded him of cinnamon mixed with vomit. Yes, definitely an unpleasant regurgitation of cinnamon flooded what was left of his throat. He coughed up bits of mold and dust.

His name had been Henry once. If his plans had been carried out properly, there was a tombstone somewhere high above that listed him as a devoted Father, Husband.

He was alive, but also dead. This was some unfortunate news. While coming to life, his bony fingers reminded him of Rice Krispies as they snapped, crackled and popped. He reached out and scratched around.

Farkleberry Forest Cemetery

Funny how people change from a person to just a body. He touched the smoothness of the top of the casket. In frustration, he kicked as hard as he could. Unfortunately, he just didn't have power in his weakened dilapidated state.

How long have I been under here? Am I supposed to be alone in here forever? I'll go crazy.

Henry heard a noise. He wasn't alone. There it was again.

Something small was climbing up his pants. He twisted and kicked until his mysterious intruder settled on his chest. Something poked up between the buttons on his dress shirt.

In the darkness, he could feel it looking at him. It was too small to be a rat, but much larger than a roach. Without much choice, Henry waited.

"Well Doodles, you gonna say hi?" a tiny voice said.

How could that be? He was alone. Surely, he was mistaken, or perhaps he had gone completely insane?

"Relax Doodles, you is as sane as the day is long. Oh yeah, you's dead all right, Doodly, but I think you's all there and even if you was crazy like ol' B.G. Stickums in the plot behind yours. I'd still like you cause you're my buddy! I decided that I'm not gonna leave your side all night long."

All night? Henry thought. What's so special about this night? What's going on?

"Doodles, c'mon its Halloweener you silly stooopids! It'stime for the dad to walk the earth, and with you beings all locked in here I thought I'd say hi."

It's not time for the dad to walk the earth.

"Did you have kids?"

Yes.

"Did you kick the bucket?"

Apparently.

"Then looks like the dad shall walk the Earth! I'm a pretty smart worm!"

Henry tried to scream with all his might, yet, when he tried, his jaw fell to the side with a creak and a thud. He tried to hold on to whatever reason he had left. You are not a worm because worms do not talk.

"Golly mister, you sure are smart! Say...you learn in people school that dead bodies wake up on Halloweener, or is that like the worms-not-talking thing?"

I'd rather not hear from you. Leave me be.

"All alone to rot by yourself? Not a chance, Doodles. I brought you the gift of stories!"

Henry felt the presence of a book being pulled on his belly.

Stories? Are they good? Henry remembered reading his favorite stories to his children as they were growing up.

"They're the best! And they's all written by the Horror Writer's Association, so you know they's good stuff."

Henry gave in to the moment and his predicament and to this charming little creature. That sounds good, he thought, as long as I'm in here I might as well be entertained by a cute little whimsical, talking worm. My grandkids would probably find you cute.

"Oh, I don't know about that, Doodles. Remember when I said I was a talking worm?"

Yes.

"I lied"

Oh.

"I'm a tapeworm, and I'm here because your organs are now working again. As I'm reading you these stories, I'm going to be feeding off your meat, Doodles. You taste so good."

No.

As the pages of the book opened and the worm read passages out loud, Henry felt the full length of this flatworm burrowing deep in his split stomach lining.

They say that to this day on Halloween, visitors standing over the grave of Henry Doodle can still hear the reading of macabre holiday-inspired tales mixed with a sucking sound and a very weak attempt to scream.

6

DEAD & BREAKFAST

A bright blinding sun rises over the dark sculpted Carpathian Mountains of Romania, where nestled deep within, there sits a tiny forgotten village. In many ways, it is still bound to its old-world traditions and customs. It's a land not seen by many from the western world, especially from travelers from the United States, for you'd have to be a world-renowned explorer to come this far. Inside a building with a sign that marks, "Happy Bed & Breakfast," an older couple sits at a table with one such traveler. This is Ma and Pa, and this is their establishment. Ma has red sad eyes as though something has gutted her happiness from the inside and she lost her smile many years before. Pa is slightly more upbeat, but he is still worn down by something dark which has taken its toll on this couple. They haven't truly been happy in a long time. It shows. Their guest sits at the table in a business suit, and he is ready to take on the day after nourishment. His mouth is stuffed with spiced meat and he motions towards his now empty glass. The old man nods and gets up in the direction of a pitcher of orange juice. He brings it back and sets it on the table. The couple knowingly locks eyes for a moment; she looks away, choosing not to see what comes next. The guest chews away, unaware of the host's glance or its meaning. From behind the suited man, Pa slips on a chokehold. A struggle ensues, and suddenly there's chaos with violent kicking and thrusting. Bits of food eject from the guest's mouth, cups knock over on the table, and Pa rams backward, nearly losing his grip in the thrusting. Pa begins to fade. The suited man looks at Ma, who avoids his gaze. She is afraid to get physically involved. Pa lets him slump in his chair, finally dead. He falls forward onto the scrambled eggs, sausage, wheat toast, and fruit.Pa falls into his chair across from Ma. She looks at him with sadness and remorse. He takes her hand in his. "I almost lost him there. Strong buck, that one," Pa says in his thick accent. "Saw that. Saw you too." Ma squeezes his hand. "You know we can't keep doing this." Pa starts to object, but ultimately agrees with her. He knows she's right. Deep down, he knows. Time catches up to us all. Pa says, "Goddamn it, you're right. It's time."

"When do we stop? How many more must we..."

"One, one more. The next guest will be the last one."

"You promise? The last one?"

Pa nods, "The last one."

Ma rests her head on Pa's shoulder, and they lightly embrace, still as deeply in love as the day they wed. They fall into an embrace, lips and tongues tangled in passion, oblivious to the dead man on their kitchen table. Later that same day, Ma changes the outdoor sign to VACANCY as Pa drags the guest to the backyard. Ma changes the linens on the bed. Pa wipes the sweat from his forehead with a gloved hand while shoveling into the earth.

The newly arrived guests exit their cabs while Ma and Pa look at each other knowingly. The two females get an eerie vibe from the bed-and-breakfast. Both girls seem nervous, but especially Annie. The house smelled of old-fashioned, dusty knitted knickknacks and doilies. Annie has dark hair, a pokey nose, and enchanting eyes. She is very excited and has a look about her like this is her birthday. Traveling from the United States across the ocean is always exciting. Visiting this land is something she's always wanted to do. Fate and circumstance has finally brought her here. The other girl, Keight has known Annie since they were young. She has blonde hair and an overall friendly disposition; she is pleased with how things are going, but she never would have come here if not for her best friend.

"So, what did you tell them?" Keight asks her longtime bestie.

"I just sent them a letter letting them know about the surprise. They don't have a phone; it's an old-fashioned kind of place."

The door opens, and the girls come face to face with Pa. He seems a bit uneasy; they were younger than what he had expected. He stares at them intensely, wondering whether he will have the strength to do what's necessary when the time came. There wasn't much fight left in his old body.

"Come on in," Pa stares intensely.

"I guess you were expecting us. It's very nice to meet you, I'm Ann—"

Pa rudely cuts her off. "This is my wife; she'll show you to your room." Pa turns and stands behind the older lady. Ma doesn't say a word; she ducks off into a room to retrieve sheets, towels, etc.

Keight whispers, "They're not very friendly."

"It's almost like they don't even want us here."

Ma leads them up to their room. An awkward silence grows with each step as they make their way up. The elderly lady finally breaks it by saying, "Its quaint, but you'll be close to town. We ask you not to have any boys over please."

"Certainly not." Annie is sincerely aghast at the thought.

"Why not?" Keight says cheerfully at the thought.

"There's been trouble in the past." Comes the reply from Pa behind them all.

Keight giggles. Her friend gives her a *cut-it-out* look.

After seeing the bedroom, Pa leads them toward the kitchen. Along the way, Annie regards the gallery of family pictures, including pictures of a baby. "Is this your grandchild?"

Ignoring Annie, Pa continues on to the kitchen.

"This is the site of some of the best cinnamon buns you'll ever have. Maybe we'll have some tomorrow." Opening the back door, they go into the yard and notice a child's play set, all alone.

Ma turns to the girls. "Oh yes, and the post you asked about, it hasn't arrived yet. Let you know as soon as it does." Annie is crestfallen but does some math in her head and is okay with it.

Annie says, "No worries, it'll be here soon enough."

Keight says, "That's a shame, but as long as we got time let's go into town."

"Shower works fine if you girls want to use it before you go out."

Sometime later, Annie is singing in the shower. Pa walks by the door with bad intentions. He turns the knob and cracks the door. Annie is behind the shower curtain. He looks as her shape through the film, and something about it doesn't feel right. Then he changes his mind and goes for the other girl. He makes his way down the hallway toward the guest bedroom. The door has no knob on it. He peers thru the hole and sees Keight as she slides a shirt over her black bra.

Pa walks in puts his hands on her. At first, she's intrigued with this stranger. She wonders where this could go; she likes older men, but then he gets rough and she twists to get away. In the struggle, her purse is knocked open, spilling its contents. She manages to grasp a knife she brought for protection. She slides it open and swings the blade, the older man is cut, yet he gets the knife from her and proceeds to cut her face. She falls and attempts to hold her face together. He swings again and again and then finishes her off with his preferred choke. He leaves the room holding his injury. The gash in his left arm leaks life's fluid.

Annie leaves the steamy bathroom. She walks the hall wearing frumpy comfy clothes and enters the guest room. She immediately sees the lifeless body of her dear friend. Danger warnings wash over Annie, causing her to turn and run. Annie runs to the kitchen in madness and despair. On the run, she can see Ma from afar.

"Oh my God, you won't believe this, I think my friend is dead. Somebody broke in..."

"Oh honey, c'mere. It's all almost over..."

When she gets up to Ma, this kindly old lady turns and brings a frying pan down on her skull. As Annie's body crumples to the hardwood floor, she thinks to herself *WHY?*

In the living room area next to the large red brick fireplace, Annie groggily came to. Through foggy eyes, she can make out the images of Ma and Pa coming into focus. She struggles before realizing she is gagged and bound to a large chair. Her struggles get her nowhere. Emotions are running high and she feels overwhelmed. Pa and Ma see she is now awake.

Pa leans forward, "I wish there had been another way but there just wasn't."

Ma adds, "You are the last one..."

"Ten years ago, we sent our daughter to America."

Ma jumps in enthusiastically, "So she can have a better life and you know, hell, I guess she did, she even had a baby; made us grandparents."

Annie can't hear this right now. She struggles and can't believe what she's hearing. She needs to communicate with them...

"Now, now. It'll be over soon."

"We opened this business, but it just didn't make enough money to be able to send to them, so we haven't seen them in over twenty years. But we still we sent the money..." Pa and Ma look at each other. "We decided to borrow our guest's possessions, tip ourselves. The first time was an accident; I got too rough with someone that didn't appreciate her cinnamon rolls." He laughs. "But then we realized it must be fate. God wants us here to help show these people it's their time to go. We don't invite them; they come of their own free will. If we can help our child at the same time, then glory be to God!"

"Glory is always to God." Ma and Pa have a strange look about them that basically says they've accepted this as good reasoning. The victim continues to moan and kick against the restraints. Pa moves in behind her. Ma looks away, distancing herself from what is indeed God's will.

"You are the last one. Take solace in that fact." Pa wraps his arms around her neck as he has done in killing so many guests over the years. There is fight left in her, but not much. She readies herself, glaring at him. "In a moment, it will all be over."

There is a knocking at the door, interrupting the moment. Ma and Pa share a glance. Pa lays a finger aside his lips and points to the window. She looks out.

"That damn nosy neighbor."

Pa relaxes a bit and puts a blanket over the girl's bound body, then opens the door while hiding what's beyond him. He steps onto the porch to talk to this intruder.

"Hello, I saw you have more renters here. That's super!"

"How can I help you?"

"Me? Oh no, no, I came to help you!" She laughs. "Got some more of your mail again, here you go." She hands a letter to Pa. "You know you are welcome to join Theodore and I for sauerkraut or cabbage rolls anytime. I can't wait to tell you about my son and his new baby, oh it's the cutest thing."

Pa nods and begins to close the door. "Well, goodbye then." She stares at the closed door.

Once inside Pa opens the letter. "Oh, my lord, it's from Mary." Ma looks up, upon hearing the name of their long-lost daughter. Pa begins to read.

> *"Mother and Father,*
>
> *I've missed you. I had so many problems as a child, and I'm only writing you this after successfully completing years of intense therapy. I'm finally at a place in my life to make amends with my past wrongs. I've fought addiction and a lot of bad choices, including leaving my homeland and avoiding family. I never wanted you to see me struggle. I've accepted the money you've sent and used it to raise your granddaughter right. In the first of many steps to heal this rift, I've sent her to you. Your guest this week, Annie is your flesh and blood. I look forward to..."*

Pa stops reading, "No, no, no!" He looks at the outline of the girl with the blanket where he left her by the fireplace. Pa is unsure what to do. Ma takes the envelope and pulls a photo from it. She shows it to Pa. It's a black-and-white photo of their visitor.

"We can explain it to her." The old man says. "Tell her it was all for her, and make amends for the loss of her friend, but at least our granddaughter is still alive." Ma sits on the couch in shock. He runs to the blanket-covered girl and places his hand on her arm. "Annie- we are so sorry. This is horrible, but we will make it up to you."

Ma starts crying uncontrollable sobs. The blanket is pulled off and for the first time Pa looks on at his granddaughter and knows why Ma is crying. Her body is still intact, but the head is beaten in, caving her skull, and she is losing an eye from the bashing. Pa noticed the frying pan lying next to the chair. Pa lost feeling in his legs and fell to his knees, joining his wife in the sobs. In the depths of despair, Ma finishes the letter.

"If my plans go correctly, I should be arriving in a day or two after Annie does,
I'll see you both soon. Please show me the same love that you did to her."

7

LIBBY

ibby decided that the next scene would be where she would stop for the night. Often engrossed in her storytelling, it was difficult to decide where to end for the evening. She typed, "The pregnant woman stood in the kitchen and heard the ghost's voice again." It was a spooky way to leave her tale envisioned for the small screen; just the way she intended. Pushing her chair back from the computer monitor, Libby smiled with unabashed glee. Squishy, a fluffy white cat, sat to her left. He had been by her side through many tough times. In a sweet way, Squishy was Libby's most loyal fan, and having him around was very comforting.

She reached out to pat Squishy on the head as he turned to his side and lightly purred. In his old age, Squishy had lost most of his spunk and his purr sounded more like a groan. Libby, getting up there herself in years, could relate. There were many days when she too had no desire to purr. Still, Libby's work kept her excited; she felt like she could live forever, as long as there were still stories to be told.

"Let's get ready for bed, eh Squishy," Libby said as she switched the computer to sleep mode. She pulled herself from the chair, and already clothed in her nightgown, she made her way to the bed where she pulled back the covers. As she settled back on the bed, Libby watched Squishy lightly paw at the covers then circle around before finally falling on the blankets with a light thud.

Libby reached across the nightstand towards her lamp that sat next to her side of the bed. She paused for a moment as her gaze fixated on a picture of herself in her younger years standing next to a man in a suit. She knew how silly she looked, being all alone in such a large bed. It had been better when Henry lay beside her. After fifty years of marriage, he had passed away just less than a year ago. Together they had been the Hollywood power couple and were talked about in all the tabloid papers which Henry had called rag mags. With his production contacts and her imagination, they had a series of successful television shows and two slightly less received movies. Libby's personal touch was that each always had a spooky element. Besides the success in tinsel town, they had raised some good children, now grown and busy raising kids of their own.

These days her life consisted of writing, talking to her family, more writing, and Squishy. Libby's hand slipped under the lampshade as she felt for the knob. Suddenly she felt something crawling across it. She let out a startled cry and quickly drew her hand back in shock. Something was moving about under the lampshade; she could see its outline through the shade. She tossed back the covers and cursed the heavens for allowing such a terrible creature to even exist. She knew what she had to do. She thought about how Henry would have handled the situation differently; he never killed anything intentionally. He would have happily scooped up the critter on a piece of paper and drop it back outside with care. She had told him on many occasions that he was like a Zen master with his "I won't kill a bug" mentality. Despite his mercy for bugs, she still loved him and missed him dearly.

Alas, being a widow, she knew that dealing with various insects was now solely her own problem. She knew she couldn't call her grown son and expect him to drive two hours down from the high desert just to simply kill a single spider, let alone make such a long trip this late in the night. Whether she liked it or not, Libby was on her own to deal with this despicable critter. She wouldn't be able to sleep soundly otherwise.

"God, what if it crawls up my nose as I sleep?" she thought to herself as she went to look for a book to squash her unwelcome guest.

Squishy watched from the bed, while Libby held a crossword puzzle dictionary in one hand and lifted the lampshade with her other. The cat made his way towards the nightstand area, and he watched from the safety of a pillow as Libby lifted the book. She wished not to come into contact with the insect for fear that its tiny bug legs would touch her aged skin. She shook the lampshade and dropped it onto the carpet. The small spider hurried out from its hiding spot, ran through her legs, and scurried halfway up the wall, passing framed awards from the world of entertainment. Finally, it rested in the corner near her bedroom door.

Libby raised the crossword puzzle book over her head and paused; she found herself studying the spider closely. Its legs gripped the wall, and although it was still a creepy disgusting thing with a fat little body, there was something about it that appeared vulnerable.

It looked at her as if to say, "Really? You're going to kill me?" Libby brought the book down as fast as she could, held it against the wall, and then pushed it back and forth just to ensure herself that the spider was completely dead. When she pulled the book from the wall, she could not believe her eyes. Although she had properly smashed the body, tiny spiders now ran from its remains.

The miniature spiders were everywhere. Libby whacked at them with her book over and over while cursing in a frantic panic. She didn't stop attacking until every last one of them was smashed. Exhaling heavily, she took some toilet paper from the bathroom and wiped up the remains. The original spider must have been carrying babies; that thought instantaneously caused coldness to creep up Libby's spine. As she gave the spider a proper toilet burial, she imagined the feel of their tiny legs all over her body and experienced a second attack of chills. On her way back from the bathroom, she ran her fingers through her white hair, half expecting to find that those tiny bastards had somehow embedded themselves into her scalp.

After everything had been taken care of, she got back in bed. This time, she left the lampshade off with the exposed bulb glaring, and she turned the knob to bring her room into the darkness. She did what she could to not disturb Squishy, who had fallen asleep during the chaos. As Libby lay in bed, her thoughts drifted back to that damn spider.

Libby looked left and right. How had she gotten up so high? It was as though she was on a skyscraper, and yet she was still somehow in her bedroom. Her many legs held tightly to the wall. She considered churning out a thin lace from her backside but decided against it; tonight was not the night. Her thoughts were on her hundreds of babies that would soon enter the world; They were her legacy. They would make her proud.

Suddenly Libby heard something stirring; her many eyes focused on the giant human lumbering in her direction. She had hoped it was that nice older gentleman who was always so very kind and sympathetic. Libby would certainly understand if he needed to place her back outside; often her curiosity caused her to wander. However, it was not the man who approached her.

"Who was this person?" Libby wondered.

She feared for herself and the lives of her unborn. She watched the white-haired woman as she lifted the book high above her head. The look on the woman's face scared Libby; she could see it in the woman's hateful eyes that there was no chance of pleading with her.

"What did I ever do to her?" Libby thought, as the book came down fast and hard.

Libby awoke screaming in her bed with tears streaming from her glassy eyes. She sat upright, trying to catch her breath. She felt so bad; how could she have killed that poor spider? She decided she needed a cup of tea to calm her nerves, but not without Squishy. Libby shook the sleeping cat until his eyes slowly opened. He followed her out of the bedroom and down the stairs. Once in the kitchen, she began feeling much better. This space of sanctuary always brought back memories of happy times and holidays. She recalled the smells of cinnamon and vanilla floating through the air as she got her teapot and readied it for the stove.

"Squishy, I had no reason to kill the little spider. I just had a terrible dream. Actually, it wasn't a dream at all; it was a horrible nightmare." Squishy curled up on a chair nearby as he licked his fur. He occasionally gazed towards her direction.

Libby continued, "It was just a spider. I'm not going to do that anymore. The next time I see something in this house that I didn't invite here, I promise I'm not ever going to kill it. I'll catch it and put it outside, just like Henry would have done."

Libby lowered the heat on the stove and poured a cup of scalding hot water. She had the tea bag and her sugar bowl already on the counter, as she had done so many times before. She looked at her loyal companion. Feeling much better about the situation in general, she blurted out, "If I kill another bug, I hope that a really big one comes and gets me!"

She couldn't help but laugh to herself as she dipped the tea bag into her cup. Watching as it stained the water, she lifted the top of the sugar bowl. For a short moment, she pictured all those tiny spiders pouring out from under the lid. They would all attack, demanding vengeance for their mother, and climb up her arms and out from under her nightgown.

Libby held her breath and scooped her sugar, feeling a wave of relief that she just had an overly active imagination. She settled back to enjoy her tea. Looking past the kitchen area, she could see the last Film and Television Awards trophy Henry had ever accepted.

She sighed and took the cup up to her lips for a sip. As she lowered it, she noticed legs dangling in front of her face—another spider! One of those daddy long legs ones that Libby had always hated; it had dropped down from the ceiling directly in front of her face.

Libby screamed and spilled her tea on the countertop, scaring Squishy in the process. The spider just hung there on its thread. It was dangling about like a skydiver whose parachute was caught in a tree. Libby could not believe her bad luck. She hadn't seen a single spider in the house since Henry had passed away.

Now, two of these wretched creatures in the very same night? It was all too much for her.

She grabbed the closest newspaper and instinctively killed the spider. When she realized what she had done Libby caught her breath and sat down. She checked her pulse to make sure she was all right, but she couldn't help but feel like a rubber band that had been stretched to its limit.

"That's it for tonight. I can't take anymore." She looked at the clock in the hallway and decided that midnight was too late to be drinking tea, anyway. She did a quick search for Squishy, but quickly gave up and walked down the hall toward the stairs. They creaked with each step as she made her way back to the bed.

Upon entering the room, Libby left the door slightly ajar for Squishy, then got into bed without turning on the light. She brushed her hands under the covers, hoping she wouldn't feel anything unwanted; she was relieved to find that there was nothing there.

A few moments later, cozy in the oversized bed and nearly asleep, she heard the pitter pat of tiny feet on the steps. As her eyes adjusted to the darkness, she saw the door pushed back and a brief moment later she felt a familiar thump on the bed. Her cat was surely pleased to finally have its master's adventure end for the night. Libby was also pleased that they could finally get their much needed rest.

Her eyes felt heavy, but before she could sleep, she began to wonder if she had left the stove on. Libby grumbled to herself, since she hadn't even cleaned up the spilled tea. What were the odds she would have—?

"Crap! Crap! Crap," she said to herself.

Libby leaped out of bed. She noticed that Squishy didn't seem to react; she reasoned that the poor old cat was probably too tuckered out to care. She reached over and gently petted him; as he let out his familiar groan-meow she was accustomed to. Some of his fur came off in her hand.

He must be shedding, she thought. *I'll have to brush him later.*

With little to no thought, she clutched the fur in her right hand as she started down the stairs. As Libby made her way down the hallway towards the kitchen, she felt light wispy filaments against her face. She was horrified to realize it was rows and rows of spider webs! Her first collected thought was to debate whether this was another nightmare, but it appeared as though she had not been to this part of the house in years. In her confused state, she entered the kitchen and flipped on the light. Her eyes found themselves on a sight that made her blood curdle.

There was a large, tangled spider web covering the farthest wall. In the center was Squishy... at least what remained of him. He'd been wrapped up in the sticky web. His innards had been sucked dry, and he was slumped over like an empty furry white sock; there was very little left of her beloved pet. Libby's mind raced for answers, trying to absorb everything, but she could only reach the chilling conclusion that this was all real. Squishy was dead, and Libby, wanting to scream but unable to do so, froze and stared into the eyes of bits and pieces of her best friend.

She thought back to how she had rubbed Squishy just before coming downstairs; how his fur had come off in her hand. Libby opened her hand to see the fur she had inadvertently grasped; instead of the snow-white fur Squishy had shed all over her house, she was now holding thin black hairs that were toppling out from her open palm. Her breath came out in short, violent bursts.

She heard something flop off her bed; she heard the many feet pitter pat on the stairs. Her heart nearly burst out of her chest. It was getting closer and closer; Libby's knees buckled, and she collapsed to the floor.

From down the hallway she could see a distorted shadow of a giant spider with its

many legs making its way slowly, very slowly, towards her.

A strong breeze blew through the window and into the hotel room and found its way from the sandy California beaches to the sleeping bodies of two newlyweds in their honeymoon suite. They were still tired from a ravenous night of passionate lovemaking. As the chill met the curves of Libby's young nude body she rolled over half asleep, half awake. Her eyes opened with shock.

She thought back to the dream, and oddly wasn't terrified, but rather perplexed by it and its implications about the future. Next to her, still sleeping with a majority of the blankets, was her new husband Henry. Both so young and full of life. She snuggled next to him and thought back to the vivid dream. From the corner of her eye, she saw movement on the far wall as something tiny ran and then stopped. She saw it and it saw her.

Then Libby shut her eyes and held onto Henry. Out her window, the Pacific Coast Highway and the City of Angels called to her with dreams of the future.

8

ADRA JO CLARK

The wind whistled in the trees and far off an owl could be heard as two people made out passionately, groping each other as though this was the last pleasure to be had. The eerie light of the full moon cast shadows on the tombstones and crosses that scattered the grassy hills of the Pennsylvania cemetery. The woman sitting on a tombstone had fiery red hair and wore a punk rocker outfit with military camouflaged pants. Adra Jo Clark was being kissed all over her neck by a blonde-haired athlete that was much larger than she, but just as turned-on. The motion of their bodies made the top portion of an unsteady monument begin to teeter, widening a crack that had grown over the many years. It looked as though it would give way completely until the jock noticed and put his hand up to steady it. They adjusted themselves so as to not knock into it again.

She fumbled with the man's belt to drop his jeans to get at what she wanted –what she needed tonight. With his pants now at his ankles, he slid his right hand along her back, under her shirt and over her bra strap. Both looked luminescent in the light of the moon, and his mouth eagerly went to hers over and over as she wrapped her legs around him. She moaned aloud with her eyes closed, feeling truly alive for the first time that day.

For as long as Adra Jo could remember, she had always loved the cemetery. There were few things in her life she did love. She certainly didn't love this varsity ass-hat she'd let pick her up from the local bar at closing time, but she thought she'd rock his world to sooth her personal demons. To Adra Jo the cemetery represented all the unexplained phenomena in the world left to be discovered, all the mysterious and the unknown. She spent a lot of time there thinking about things, like what happens to us when we die. She was sure some part of us lived on, but she didn't like the answers she got from small town churches.

Blah Blah Blah God is good... pass the collection plate, see you sinners next Sunday. Adra Jo was bored of the every day, the average, and the boring life she saw all around her. She had always hoped and dreamed for something more, something *exciting*, and something that would shake up her life.

The jock's hands fumbled with her right breast. Her eyes were closed as she ran her tongue along his neck. Then she opened her mouth wide and bit the athletic man as hard as she could. He winced as a trickle of blood ran down his shoulder; he pulled away to look at her. She gave him a slightly playful look in return. "The fuck! The guys were right. You are a freak!" he exclaimed.

She smiled a wicked little smile and licked the blood from her tongue. It tasted metallic. The pain didn't diminish his interest in the heaven she had to offer between her legs, and gradually they fell back into each other's arms, dancing the dance of lovers with Adra Jo licking at his injured neck. With half-opened eyes, she noticed a figure standing off in the distance. Somebody was watching them.

"Slow down." She mumbled. "Someone's coming."

"Yeah, me; I'll be cumin round the mountain when I cum."

"No, somebody's watching us."

He turned towards the figure and hollered in an authoritarian tone that was known to scare underclassmen anywhere he went, "Hey, what the fuck are you looking at, you perv? Get outa here!"

With the mood momentarily broken, this time it was Adra Jo who pulled away from him.

"It's fine babe, seriously my dad's a cop. The cops run this town. Don't worry? Nobody's not gonna do shit." In the distance, the person didn't stop approaching and was eerily closer now, and it became clear that it was indeed the outline of a female. On closer inspection, he was the first to notice it was a naked woman. She had attractive features for most of her body, large breasts that bounced with each of her steps towards their direction, swaying hips, and between her long legs she was unshaved. The thought occurred to Adra Jo that perhaps this woman was on her way to a nineteen-seventy's porno shoot.

The jock turned to his redheaded love interest and said, "It must be my lucky night, is this one of your freaky friends?"

Adra Jo Clark just looked past him at the oncoming person, who was now looking less like a woman and more like something else entirely.

The woman revealed her monstrous hands that were previously hidden behind her back. As she did, Adra Jo saw that she had unshaved armpits to match her unkempt vulva hair. Her long brown hair on her head hid her pointy long ears, and her mouth hung open due to an ungodly overabundance of fangs with two especially large ones featured in the front. The creature made animal noises and had an angry look in her bright yellow glowing eyes. When the she-beast got too close to the couple, Adra Jo hopped off the tombstone and rushed to the creature. Her mind was a jumble of questions.

Is this some kind of prank? Is she wearing a mask? Why is she naked? And last but not least in her mind: Could this possibly be a real ghoul or vampire?

As long as she could remember it was her dream to find proof that there was a world outside of our understanding. Could this female finally be her answer? When she got within range of the deformed visitor, she didn't get time to ask it any questions before it snarled at her and bared the fangs in a very unladylike move. The blood vessels on the creature's head and neck showed up a bright blue and pulsed on the edge of her skin as she snarled at the girl in the army outfit.

Adra Jo took her jacket off and offered it to the naked man beside her, "You cold?"

The man was not amused, noticed that his pants were still at his ankles, and shouted, "It's probably a mask or some shit. Hey, what does it want?"

As Adra Jo turned to look at him, the creature swatted back a thunderous right hand, knocking Adra Jo off her feet, and sending her tumbling backwards down the wet grassy hill. As she rolled out of sight of the beastly woman, Adra Jo saw glimpses of it lunging for the jock. With its large outstretched hands, it looked like the monster hit him in the chest, knocking him over the tombstone. Adra Jo stopped rolling and hit the bottom, and her right leg splashed in the cool wet water of the stream that ran through the cemetery. Her head hit the rocks along the edge; blackness crept in all around her. She had to fight the urge not to pass out from the impact.

Her hands went to her face to feel the damage. Her nose hurt like hell and was bleeding bad; she knew it might be broken. This wouldn't be the first time she'd had her nose broken. *What to do now? I should get the hell out of here!* She looked up at where she'd fallen from. It looked so very far away now.

At the top of the hill, she heard muffled sounds of the jock as he was attempting to scream. She forced herself up to her feet slowly, and she noticed the fallen leaves stuck to her wet camouflaged pants. The blood from her face ran into the water. *That bitch can't get away!*

As she made her way back up the grassy hill, she heard the sounds of the man getting louder. His wails were being replaced with the ungodly sounds of ripping flesh and tearing organs. Adra Jo kept her eyes open for any other *thing* that might have wandered on by tonight. *Perhaps a werewolf or a goblin too,* she thought to herself. *Am I going crazy?*

When she reached a set of tombstones near the scene where she could view what was going on, she ducked down behind it quickly, not wanting to be seen. *This is really happening, not in a movie somewhere, but this is actually happening to me.* Squatting on the wet grass and her heart thumping wildly in her chest, she looked out at the horrific scene.

The she-beast was on all fours on top of the man. Her ass was in the air and her face was buried down by his crotch. Adra Jo thought, *why is she blowing him? That cock was mine.* She quickly dismissed the thought, thinking that if it was the case, it must be the worst blow job of all time because blood ran over the grass in a huge ever-growing puddle. As she watched from a distance, the creature's head rose from his midsection with various entrails in its fanged mouth. Organs and intestines squished and slid along his torn-up middle as his body shook on the grass, clearly in shock. Hunks of flesh and stomach were spit from her fanged mouth as she dove back in for more. It reminded her of that fat fuck Larry Urbas bobbing for apples last Halloween.

The man's head turned to the side, his eyes meeting Adra Jo's. As a look of shock and fear ran over his face, he mouthed the words, *help me.* Alas, she looked on helplessly as his body finally stopped fighting. She felt sick. She figured most people that love horror movies are desensitized to this kind of shit, but she barely managed to ingest the vomit back down that arose up in her throat. As her insides burned from swallowing it, she noted the smell in the air. Over the years, she'd grown used the sight of the occasional deer hung split open by a hunter with its entrails emptied out on the lawn. In northwestern, Pennsylvania, hunting was a way of life. This putrid smell was far worse. It was a mix of bile and excrement. Suddenly, the smells of death and dying were all around her.

While the beast continued feeding on her date, Adra Jo thought about her next move. She had no interest in being the next to be dissected. *What to do? What to do?* She noticed the nearby cemetery monument that earlier in their activities had appeared to be not so sturdy. Parts of the religious symbol still looked ready to fall off if somebody would just hit it hard enough. Without thinking too much about it and hoping her feet wouldn't slip on the wet grass as she sprinted, she made a mad dash for the monument. As she ran by the carnivore, it turned its head to see her; its face was now a crimson mask with bright yellow eyes and a nose that took in deeply the smell of fresh meat. Its curious eyes followed her body as Adra Jo hit into the loose structure with all her might. The beast barely had a moment to fathom what was happening before the top of the monument came down across its legs, pinning it to the ground with a powerful smash.

The predator let loose a powerful scream and began to rip at the boulder with his long fingers. When it finally stopped clawing and accepted that it was trapped, it angrily looked at her and hurled the head off of the jock, sending it flying in her direction. The fleshy skull hit the tombstones near her and rolled next to her.

The creature's tantrum continued as it pounded the body of the man with its heavy fists. Adra Jo walked closer to it, feeling safe now that it was trapped facedown by the concrete structure.

"Can you speak? Do you understand me? I always knew that you existed out there somewhere, no matter what people said." She looked at its face and saw that there were no signs of understanding. Adra Jo continued talking aloud, "You're not a zombie and too real to be a ghost..." She looked at the blood all around her and uttered the word as a question, "Are you a Vampire?"

It rested itself on its elbows and turned toward the direction of this clever redhead it had encountered. It first glared at her and then began to smile at her. The grin was wide enough to show bits of flesh still hanging off its teeth.

It hissed back at her proudly flexing its confidence to hunt. If it had ever been human, that was a long time ago.

When Adra Jo looked into its eyes, she saw such intensity inside them. There was such anger and a wildness, and it kept her from getting too close.

Adra Jo wished it could speak, because she had so much she wanted to learn from her captor. There were so many questions circling in her mind about who this is, or at least who it used to be? *Why was it here now? Was there more like her out there, perhaps in the darkness yet to be discovered?*

Adra Jo didn't get a chance to ask anything, because this brief shared moment was brought to an end as soon as the creature noticed the sky behind the trees of the cemetery was suddenly lit up with the first signs of a new day. Sunlight was coming soon. The animalistic rage intensified, and it clawed at the monument frantically. It looked at the morning sky again and clawed some more. Finally, it looked at Adra Jo with fear in its eyes for the first time.

The sunlight, Adra Jo thought. *Of course, it hates the sun; if it's a vampire, it'll burn in the light and die, classic vampire trait. Everyone knows that. Damn.*

In one swift motion, the vampire took its right hand and tore into its neck with all the fingers breaking open the flesh. With that one fluid motion, it had torn its own throat out, spraying the blood and bits all over Adra Jo. A thought went through Adra Jo's mind. *This blood I'm being sprayed with belonged to the jock. Gross.*

As the red-haired woman covered her eyes from this explosion of vital fluids, it was suddenly all over. She dropped to her knees in front of this macabre sight. *Fuck.* Whatever it was; it was dead now, lying on top of the headless body of her earlier fling. He'd only wanted to hookup and now he was dead. How's this for the consequences of sin? Adra Jo clenched her hands into fists and screamed at the dead vampire, as the first rays of sun cast their light over the cemetery.

"Noooo!" Adra Jo screamed. "You can't leave me. I had to know that there's more to life than THIS!"

After the anger slightly subsided, she watched for the inevitable; the creature's naked body fully igniting in some sort of internal combustion that was always in the movies. She waited, and she waited for the fires.

It never came. The body just lay there on top of the jock.

That was odd.

Adra Jo started pacing back and forth, looking again and again at the bodies, trying to decide what to do next. She knew she could call the cops, after all there were two dead bodies… kind of. Well, at least one. At least the human one counted.

She ran her fingers through her long red hair full of flesh pieces, wiped blood from her face and she let out a breath. *Who to call? What to do?* Suddenly realization washed over her like a calming breeze. She keyed in a number saved on her cell phone for if the right day ever came along, and it began to ring...

"Hello, TMZ tip line..."

Holy shit, I'm going to be famous.

9

LET'S GET READY . . . TO LET THE HEADS ROLL

Wrestling and Horror have a long tradition of meeting in the ring.
Originally published in
Fangoria Magazine Issue 345 Released Nov. 2015
Cowritten by John Palisano

A bell rings as smoke fills the arena. Flashes of lightning appear on the large Titantron screen high above the thousands of fans in attendance. Either watching in person or at home on pay-per-view, fans know it's going to be another match with a macabre finish—it might be hangings, body bags, burying someone alive or even a classic casket match. These theatrics have replaced the steel cages that were once so prevalent. Chills pass through the crowd. Fans raise their lighters like they're at a heavy metal concert. Children gasp as a short, chubby man in a suit steps through the mist holding an urn to his chest and cries, "Oh, yes!" This man is known to the fans as Paul Bearer and his appearance signifies the arrival of the WWE phenomena: The Deadman …The Undertaker. Will tonight be one of his infamous 'Hell in a Cell' matches?

Even though the amazing popularity of the Undertaker is certainly not the first time horror imagery and wrestling have come together, his impressive presence in pop culture and huge success for promoters all over the world has inspired many wrestling stars to adopt horror elements to their characters, reaching past the common convention of generic Babyfaces versus Heels, or good guys versus bad guys. The era of the super hero urging you to say your prayers and eat your vitamins is passé, replaced with an unforgettable Demon who's been summoned from the depths of a lake, or an evil leprechaun, or worse. Recently, [REDACTED] was lucky enough to speak with some Main Event wrestlers currently touring the world. A Demon, a Snake, and a Boogey Man speak about the past, the present, and the future of the collision between wrestling and horror.

Sinn Bodhi, former WWE wrestler better known as Kizarny, a crazy carnival freak, says: "I can train in the gym all day long. It's just not going to make me seven feet tall. The Undertaker is an ominous man in stature, so if he comes out all serious—with the right regalia—with the music, and the lighting—it sets an awesome tone. Whereas Gangrel (*a famous vampire wrestle*) is medium sized, I'm no midget, but for wrestling I'm pretty small at 6'2" and 230 pounds—that's runty for a heavyweight wrestler. Gangrel is about 6'3" and just shy of 300 pounds, while The Undertaker is 6'10" and is easily 300 pounds. I'm the faster of the three, which is my plus. I don't come out trying to look all serious. My ambience is really scary because I'm mixed with really cute imagery. I've got bloody, angry stuff going on, but then? I've got duckies and bunnies strapped to me. I'm Psycho. I've got circus animals hanging off me. I can't tell you how often fans come up to me and say how they never thought pink hearts and duckies would be so scary. Women tell me that I'm the creepiest performer they've ever seen in the ring and tough guys that think they could take me are afraid I'll bite their faces off!" Sinn currently runs Freakshow Wrestling, and was recently honored by the prestigious Cauliflower Alley Club in Las Vegas, inducted by legendary madman wrestler Jake the Snake Roberts.

Jake the Snake, known for his eloquent promos as biting as the snakes he took inside the ring, was even once assisted at WrestleMania 3 by none other than horror rocker Alice Cooper. Jake is unfortunately also widely known for his personal horrors of drug and alcohol abuse, as documented in the 1999 film *Beyond the Mat*. Jake says he's much better these days. He says, "Getting sober was the first step." Jake was recently inducted into the WWE Hall of Fame, and we couldn't be happier for him. We caught up with Jake after a live wrestling event in Hollywood, where he was victorious over Scorch the Clown. "I wrestled the Undertaker at WrestleMania 8, and you want to know my thoughts on horror in pro wrestling? It's all about the mystique of horror. What is it? What's it come from? The bump underneath the bed? Or what's in the closet? That's what it's all about. Horror. Scaring kids. Wrestling does that."

When asked about the most iconic horror characters in wrestling, Jake replied, "Well, I think Mankind—the original Mankind—before he went silly on everybody. Mankind was pretty spooky." Mankind lived inside a boiler room, collected, body parts, and wore a signature Hannibal Lector-style mask. He would rock back and forth, s creaming for his 'mommy' while pulling clumps of his hair out.

Backstage before yet another live wrestling event we caught up with former WWE wrestler The Boogie Man as well as the lovely Katarina Leigh Waters (formerly known as the WWE Diva Katie Lea Burchill) before a live wrestling event. When asked about the fan reaction to The Boogey Man he said, "As I see you, you see me. As I look into the mirror I'm a part of you and you are a part of me." He lets out a characteristically evil laugh. "They love it!

Katarina spoke about her time fighting against Boogey in WWE. "Standing in the ring and hearing that music and having him come out—the dance and the smoke, the laughter—it was probably the most exciting thing I did while I was there. I wish it'd lasted a little bit longer."

The Boogey Man is known for actually eating handfuls of live worms, as well as throwing them into the audience, scattering fans in all directions. Given the chance, we had to ask the man about the creepy crawlies. "The worms weren't the only thing, but were was the easiest to control. I had insects: maggots, Madagascar roaches, crickets, and so forth, in my pouch, but the only thing they could control was the worms. When we went into the arena we'd have to pay an infestation clause of $80,000, so they didn't want to do that. I must add working with Kat was the most phenomenal time. One of the highlights of my career. She's a very good, professional wrestler, her and Paul Burchill. We had a good thing—a good feud—and I wish it would have lasted longer, but you know what? That memory of her and Paul … is something I'll take with me to my death."

What about the elements of his act that scare people? The voodoo? The supernatural? The creature in the closet, sprinkled with a little bit of magic—how did it all come together for him? "Boogey Man has been here since the beginning of time. All cultures have it, and it's a part of everyone." Katarina added, "The reason why the Boogey Man caught on so much, and lasted so long, is because he's not a stereotype. It's grown out of you—evolved out of you—native roots and voodoo. It's more than a two dimensional character. It's quite magical. It's not like you're acting. You feel like you're interacting with a creature."

When the topic of horror arises, few have been as big in the WWE in the last decade as Gangrel, otherwise known as The Vampire Warrior. From his entrance rising up through a circle of fire, to his evil group of minion wrestlers known as the Brood, to spitting blood out of a goblet into the air before a match, this fanged man is born of darkness. He even began his career as a member of the Undertaker's group: The Ministry of Darkness. When you've got a wrestler whose finishing move is *The Nail in the Coffin*, we knew we had to catch up with the vampire. He spoke at the Art Parlor in Valley Village, California, after a night of wrestling-themed spoken word. "I wrestled originally as Lestat. Then when I toured Puerto Rico and became the Vampire Warrior. It's easier to be a Heel. Faces are usually jerks—biggest jerks in the business. Heels are awesome and they're actually the nice guys." Looking at his fanged face dripping blood onto his renaissance-era fluffy, white shirt, we couldn't agree more. Gangrel still tours regularly at various championships all over the world.

D'lo Brown is a longtime WWE performer and former Intercontinental Champion, as well as the longest member of The

Nation of Domination, with matches against Stone Cold, The Rock, and more. When asked about horror in the squared circle had this to say: "A good horror wrestling character is someone that invokes fear, like Freddy Krueger or Michael Myers. That immediately brings you to Kane (the Undertaker's evil brother), Gangrel, the Undertaker, Edge, and Christian. These were characters that invoked that fear in you— that element of: I don't want to be in the middle of a horror movie."

When asked if the performers need to have a darker side to themselves in real life or just be a good performer overall, D'lo lit up. "It's a little bit of both. Wrestling characters are a little bit about yourself but then [a performer] magnifies what you are even if you aren't. I know Kane, and he's not a scary guy but he really comes off that way." We go on to chat about the early WWE character the evil dentist, Isaac Yankum DDS, which Glen Jacobs, the man behind the Kane gimmick, had performed. D'lo had this to say: "The Dentist invokes a different type of fear."

Glen Jacobs would go on to play the evil killer Jacob Goodnight in the horror film *See No Evil*, with *See No Evil 2* having just wrapped principal photography.

Recently, more of these larger-than-life monsters have crossed over to mainstream film. To get a better look at the transition of professional wrestlers to film, we met with David DeFalco, director of *Chaos*, the movie Roger Ebert called, "ugly, nihilistic, and cruel," and what some might believe is the most brutal movie in history. DeFalco directed both former WWE World Heavyweight Champions Rob Van Dam and Batista in their first co-starring film outside of wrestling. Here's what he said of discovering Batista, years before he his breakout success playing Drax the Destroyer in *Guardians of the Galaxy*. "In the case of Batista, many wrestlers get the chance to succeed, but only two get to the height of The Rock and Batista. I had a direct participation in that I wrote direct, produced, and directed his first movie. The Rock isn't a great actor, but is a good actor. They have the larger than life charisma, and can translate that to the big screen. I clearly saw that ability in Dave. In order to be successful, they've got to know their limitations, and put themselves in the right vehicle."

The right vehicle for so many these days is to take a walk on the wild side and not run from your shadow, but embrace it, and walk with it. Last year's WrestleMania had Bray Wyatt taking on The Undertaker, as well as The Icon Sting, in main event matches. Horror and professional wrestling will always attract die-hard fans, be it on television, or in sold out arenas and stadiums. But, as we're seeing, these characters and performers are crossing over to mainstream success in a major way. As D'Lo brown put it, "It's [all] a bit of being a performer and tapping into it and bringing out the best of yourself." See you ringside!

"I think that this film will be the ultimate, because not only do we have the sensibility of the aliens and predators and all that, but we have the sense of humor that goes along with it.... and we have nudity and gore –"

I mean... WHAT DO YOU WANT IN A FILM FOR CRYING OUT LOUD???!!!"

— Del Howison, Bram Stoker award-winning author and the co-owner of *Dark Delicacies*, a brick and mortar horror-themed shop in Burbank, California

10

NIGHT OF THE NAKED HUNTER

BASED ON THE SCREENPLAY "NAKED ALIEN MASSACRE"

The sun set behind the trees of the rustic hidden resort. Past empty volleyball courts and pool areas, scientists with various beeping gadgets investigated the lands. Beeps and blips started to go off at an alarming rate, which caused Dr. Robyn Chambers to turn to her fellow scientists, Farnsworth and Beguile.

Chambers exclaimed, "See, I told you, look at the radioactivity here. It's not just radioactivity, its Technetium. This could be the scientific find of our generation. Everything changes here, right now, in these woods. Let's gather as many samples as we can to take back to the lab."

The scientists then started debating the implications of how this changed things in the scientific community. As the discussion went on, a little creature waddled out and made itself seen to the people with the clipboards. It was an adorable, pink furry creature with big Disney'esq blinky eyes and eyelashes. It hopped on a log and looked at them inquisitively.

Dr. Chambers leaned forward to look it over, "Oh my god, what is that?"

"Looks like one of those 1980s Care Bears," came the reply from Farnsworth.

The accompanying two male scientists began to move towards it, but Chambers held them back, taking charge of the situation as she has been known to do.

Chambers directed, "This could be us making first contact with a new race, so follow my lead."

Robyn leaned down to talk to it. "Can you understand me?"

The little pink Jim Henson reject just stared at them all and blinked its large watching eyes. Suddenly, it began to scrunch up its furry tiny face and push. It looked like it had gas, and all at once bubbles began to come out of its body and rise into the air.

"Miraculous. Don't be scared, we won't hurt you," Robyn Chambers tried to sound convincing.

As the small group gathered around it, the bubbles began to pop and fizz all around the scientists. Suddenly there was carnage and screaming from the men. Robyn stumbled back, unsure of the new feeling that was coming over her. She lost all sense of time and didn't know if she stood a minute or an hour. She only watched as horrible endings for those scientists she knew so well flashed around her. Stomachs were being torn open by long tentacles, bodies broken over a giant creature's knee amid screaming, and evil demonic horribleness flashed. She was surrounded by damnation, evilness, blood, and fire. There was nothing funny, and yet she laughed uncontrollably at the surrealness of it all.

Robyn noticed that all of her clothes had been ripped off her body. She was fully nude except for her boots and a scarf around her neck. She shook off the evil haze around her thoughts and ran for safety, but just as she thought she had broken free something grabbed her and pulled her quickly off into the darkness. She felt like she was swallowed by pure madness. She screamed

The trees sway in the breeze, and the wilderness with mountains all around became as it was before the men of science had appeared. A little pink being shuffles off into the brush.

The alarm clock went off. Allair Buck jumped out of bed and started putting on clothes over the modest attire she slept in. She was late for her Drawing 2 class.

She quickly grabbed her art supplies, including a canvas holder with a strap that went around her neck. On her way out, she stopped briefly to apply makeup to her young face. As she made a quick adjustment to her blonde locks, the door opened and in walked Emily McGuinness, Allair's roommate. Allair was grateful for Emily's charming company. Emily was still wet from the shower, and she wore a towel comfortably around her body; her dark skin glistened with drops of water.

In her properly spoken Queen's English Emily exclaimed, "Oh, bloody hell... You're still here? You better hurry, you're going to be late for your lovah."

"He's not my LOVAH." Allair passed Emily in the doorway on her way out.

"Not yet." Emily said under her breath. Allair can't believe she said that.

"Is today the day you'll finally talk to him about something other than tater tots?"

"Dunno, maybe... Gotta go! Love you!" Allair quickly shut the door.

"Love you too."

As she sat in the circle of art students, Allair sketched with charcoal the image of a nude male. She shaded the curves of his body nicely. Janet leaned in. "I wish I could see what you're seeing. I'm not getting that at all," she said.

Allair was slightly embarrassed and annoyed with Janet's comment.

"Oh, really?" Allair attempted to take the attention off of her. "How's yours coming along?"

Janet sighed, "I don't think I have enough charcoal to capture this beast in all its glory. That monster casts a big shadow."

Ms. Fraga, the art instructor, snuck up on them. "Does it now? Keep your eyes on your own work, Janet, and Allair I need you to focus on the model you currently have in front of you. Not your imagination."

An obese nude female was posed on her side in front of the class. She was laid out on a wooden table with a red cloth between her rolls and the hickory.

"Yes, ma'am," Allair sheepishly replied.

"Our male nude shows up in the second hour, but true to your prediction, it will indeed be Matt again." The instructor moved on to critique other students.

"Can you imagine looking like that? I wouldn't leave my house, let alone lay out in front of strangers," Janet whispered.

"Takes a lot of courage, I guess."

"Fuck, that doesn't happen overnight, that takes a lot of cake and donuts, that's what it takes, it's just disgusting. I didn't even know you could order extra powder on donuts." Janet chuckled and went back to her drawing. Allair looked at Janet, then the model, and took everything in. This is the world she lived in. She sighed.

"Okay class, that's a break. Our next model will be here in a few minutes," the art teacher announced loudly.

The plus sized model gathered her things and dropped a shoe near Janet. As she reached for it, Janet retrieved it.

Janet, with all the fake sincerity in the world, said, "Oh, here you go dear, and from one woman to another let me just say how much I admire your courage to get up there."

Allair was shocked, and she walked from her drawing easel towards the doorway with disgust. She stared off the hallway and waited for a glimpse of *him* as he came to class. Ms. Fraga noticed and motioned for Allair to approach. "Spending a lot of time drawing Matt Stanton, aren't you?"

"You noticed?" Allair attempted to sound aloof.

"Honey, a blind man would have noticed. You draw him even when he's not around."

Allair's face flushed red.

The teacher continued, "Its fine, just please when you're in class focus on what's at the moment in front of you from here on. But as long as we're talking about him, you do have good taste. Matt is a charming boy. I've known him and the Stantons for a long time. They are all good people."

Allair eagerly digested her words.

"So, you've been going to lunch with him, lately?" The teacher pried.

"Twice so far. We don't talk much, but he seems like a nice guy. I guess I'm just a fan."

"Well, I think you two could make a wonderful couple."

Allair blushed again. "Maybe these lunches will blossom into something else. You never know." Allair happily walked away.

Just then a good-looking, well-cut model showed up ready to pose with just his robe and slippers on. The instructor greeted him.

"Hello, Matt. How's life treating you? How are things? Is Teddy doing well these days?"

"Things are super, and you know how Teddy is. Teddy is Teddy, but I can tell that he really misses having you around."

"Well, I miss him too, but there are some things that go on over there that I can't really be a part of." There is a brief moment of contemplation and understanding between the two that has the potential of growing uncomfortable, before she continues talking. "So anyway… today we'll begin with some gestures and lead into longer poses as class goes on. Good?"

"You're the boss, Boss. Is Allair already in there?"

"Yes, she is. Funny you should ask. We were just talking about you. She mentioned how you two have been going to lunch lately."

"Anything else she said?" He attempted to sound cool.

"I think there might be something more there besides friendship. Are you interested in something more, Matt?"

Matt nodded, "We'll see; there's still some stuff she doesn't know about me."

The instructor smiled and turned to begin the class. Allair moved her backpack and all her art supplies away as far from Janet as she could get. Janet looked on, offended.

Ms. Fraga began, "Class, we are going to begin with gestures. These will only be for a second or so, get the gist of the form quickly."

Matt removed his robe, revealing his fully nude form, and stepped up on the platform. He struck his first pose of the day. Standing like the Heisman trophy statue, he purposefully avoided Allair's eyes. The instructor walked around the class and observed the students' work.

"Please do draw what's in front of you and remember that in art as well as in life to always keep an open mind. SWITCH!"

Matt took a new pose, and this time his eyes met Allair's. He smiled, and she returned the smile.

Allair was so happy and excited. She was holding the blue robe that the male model had on earlier and she stopped to fall against the wall. She felt so high. She could not believe what happened. It was the greatest day of her young life. Kinda! She opened the door to her dorm room, and Allair fell on her bed. Her roommate Emily noticed how ecstatic she was.

"Oh, dear, what the hell happened?"

"Emily! I'm an idiot!" Allair hid her face with her pillow.

"Yes, I know... is there a naked man in the hall with his willy flopping about shouting, 'Who took me robe?'"

"Here's what happened. I finally talked to him. I mean, like REALLY talked to Matt."

"Ahh, naked Matt." Emily grinned.

Allair Buck ignored her and continued, "So we were having lunch after class."

"And then..."

"You had lunch again with naked Matt?"

Allair was excited to be talking about this.

"Did you have wieners for lunch? Ding-dongs for desert?" Emily teased her roommate.

Allair ignored her and continued, "SO WE WERE HAVING LUNCH AND..."

Allair told the story about earlier that same day. Once class was over and Allair was eating at the dining hall with male model Matt, still wearing the robe from earlier. They talked and laughed. There was something going on behind both their eyes. There was a chemistry the other people around them noticed.

Allair started the conversation, "So, I can't believe you are comfortable doing that. I could never be nude in front of so many strangers."

"Oh, you get used to it. A job's a job. It has its perks. Hey, I got to meet you. So, do you have a job while you're in school?"

"No, I thought about it, but decided I'll be a full-time student for now."

Matt shifted in his chair, "Are you majoring in art? I don't think I ever asked you."

"No, I'm just taking a minor in drawing. There's no real money in art, so I'm an English major, I'm going to be become a teacher."

"Oh, that's right, I think you may have told me that before. So, how's the drawing coming along? Do you feel like you're getting a lot out of the class?"

It was Allair's turn to change positions in her chair, "No, um, I don't know. It's just a hobby, really. I'm not sure. It's kind of like 'La La land' in there, you know?"

Matt looked quizzically at Allair, "I don't follow. What's like 'La La Land'?"

"Where else can you walk in and see a naked person standing in the middle of the room like nothing is going on. You don't see that in regular life."

Matt chuckled, "You do in a locker room."

"First of all, mister, there's nobody in there drawing every intricate curve of my bodice, and-and second of all..." Allair suddenly felt very exposed as she continued. "I don't even get naked in the locker room, anyway."

"You don't get unclothed, why is that?"

"It's embarrassing. Not everyone has a perfect body."

Just then Matt got a text message. He looked at it and became slightly upset.

"Oh, it's my ride. Looks like I'll be hanging out in the cafeteria for another hour. My friend is fighting with her boyfriend again." Allair saw the opportunity and finally made her move. "Matt, do you need a ride somewhere? Because if you're waiting for a ride... I do have a car."

Matt looked up brightly. "You don't mind," he asked.

She really didn't mind. Both were a little nervous., The ride home was the first time they were alone together.

Allair tried to sound casual, "So, you live around here?"

"Just a few hours away."

"Hours?" Allair considered how late it'd be when she got back to the dorms.

Matt laughed, unable to keep a straight face. "I'm kidding, its right outside of town. It's not too far, you're not stuck with me for too long."

"It's not that I really don't mind." She attempted to flirt, knowing that she could spend forever with him. "I look forward to Tuesdays now, I-I like seeing you." She was happy she said it. It felt like a weight had been lifted, but then she caught what she said and how it could be taken. "I mean, not seeing you naked, I meant talking to you. I-I didn't mean your PENIS." Her face scrunched at the word PENIS, and suddenly Allair wished she was anywhere but in the car next to the man she has a crush on.

"Hey, it's okay. It's okay. I understand." Matt attempted to break the tension. Allair seemed slightly relieved, but only slightly.

"I guess you kinda have to look at it to draw it; make sure the shading is just right."

Allair was slightly uncomfortable. "You're teasing me now."

"Well, you brought it up," Matt chuckled.

"I brought your penis up."

Matt smiled, "You always do."

They sat in the awkward silence as the car drove on. Eventually they passed a sign for a family-friendly nudist resort, The Bare Bear.

"You are acting like such a weirdo perverted freak show. Maybe I should drop you off there so you can be with your kind." She stuck her tongue out at him.

"Don't know about that, I might be over-dressed in this robe. Actually, if you could take a right up here." Matt instructed.

They pulled off onto a dirt road and sat in silence a moment before Allair offered, "There's a lot of wilderness out here, do you ever go hiking?"

"Sure, I go hiking all the time. Why last summer a friend and I hiked up to Blackwell Falls. It was so nice to get away from everything and everybody else."

Allair replied, "I know what you mean. Sometimes I just want to get in my car and drive away to the middle of nowhere."

"There really is nothing like being off the grid for a couple of days," Matt countered.

"There's a modern-day philosopher I look up to, Robert Pirsig, who wrote about 'The Giant' in society, who reaches his tentacles out to ensnare us all. It traps us in a life full of fakery, that stuff that everyone says we need to be happy. I feel like when I can get away from cities. I'm avoiding his grasp for a little while longer."

Matt blinked, "Wow, that's really deep."

"Just something I'm into. He's an epically rad guy, you should look him up. He wrote that famous Zen book about motorcycles, but I think his next book was by far the best."

"So, 'The Giant' is a bad guy?"

"Yes. Conforming to what society says is okay is always a bad thing." Allair was glad that he was interested.

Matt rolled down the window and screamed out the window, "Well, fuck you giant!" They laughed together as they shared this moment.

After the laughter died out, Matt instructed, "Oh, I live just up ahead on the left."

"Yikes, you live really close to orgy central. Don't you ever get worried that one of those fat kid-touchers are gonna come over and offer you a roofie-colada?"

Matt chuckled, "Or maybe a date-rape daiquiri; I don't really have that problem, and surprisingly it doesn't bother me."

"Have you ever seen any of these freaks walking around? I can't even imagine the kind of person who would go to a place like that." Allair was a little surprised at her own prejudice.

They passed a sign that welcomed them to The Bare Bear.

Matt announced, "Okay, this is my stop."

"No! C'mon stop it. Where do you really live?"

Matt exhaled. "Allair, I live here. My family lives here. Most of my friends live here too. I'm a nudist."

Allair was beyond shocked. All the blood drained from her face. She couldn't talk if she wanted to.

Matt explained, "We have a lot of fun." Allair just nodded, muffled by her own earlier stupidity. She was tremendously embarrassed.

Matt continued, "I have friends coming over this weekend as a matter of fact. We are doing some camping and partying. You should join us."

Allair forcibly willed herself to speak, "Okay," Allair stared blankly.

"Great! So it's decided then! You'll have fun and meet some great people. Nude isn't lewd!"

Matt got out of the car and started to walk away. He stopped suddenly and remembered something; he quickly returned to the car. Could you drop this off at the art department for me?" Matt took off his robe and stood naked next to her car. He attempted to pass the covering to her. She didn't take it, and finally he just tossed it on the passenger seat.

"So, I'll pick you up this Friday! Early! We don't want to lose any sun!" At the sound of his voice, Allair slowly came to life and drove back toward sanity as fast as she could.

As Allair finished her story Emily chose to quip, "You don't even fancy anyone sees you in your knickers and now you'll be taking them off." Allair was flabbergasted as the realization hit her. She screamed into her pillow.

Allair's muffled voice sounded from the bedding, "I KNOW!! What am I doing?"

"I'll tell you what you're doing. You're getting sun burnt in places you never dreamed."

Poking out from under her pillow, Allair muttered, "I can't do this, I'm going to cancel."

Emily interjected, "You're being daft. Live a little. For God's sakes, you're not your brother!"

Allair paused, "Yes, William." She turned to a picture of him being overly religious, holding a bible tight to his chest like his baby. He was wearing a white robe. "He always knows just what to do."

"Then why doesn't he ever do anything besides pray?" Emily folded her arms indignantly.

Emily shrugged, "He's not that bad."

"Yes, he is."

"He's probably somewhere right now praying for your soul." Allair responded to that remark with a strong look. Emily has seen it before. "Fine, this Friday you are going to go and get naked with the man of your dreams." Allair smiled, feeling happy for a moment. It was only a moment until Emily continued, "... and his family. And his friends and strangers you don't know at all."

Allair was not happy anymore. She screamed and covered her face under blankets and pillows. Emily was encouraged by Emily's reaction and continued to egg her on. "Here a willy, there a willy, everywhere a willy…"

Lost deep in the woods near the Bare Bear sat an old-fashioned giant television set with a screen full of static. The ominous place did not welcome visitors. Dragging something, a figure walked by the creepy TV screen; it was possibly a bear trap. As he passed the TV screen, he hit the top with his fist and caused the static to stop long enough for a program to come into play. The images were distorted, weird images of violence and death. Clearly a psycho lived here.

Inside the college residence building, Allair sat waiting for the adventure. She resigned herself to the journey. Be it a good one or a bad one. She was nervous for the unknown. A car pulled up with a sign on it which read, "THE BARE BEAR." Matt was driving, and a skinny Asian man sat next to him. Allair waved at Matt and walked to the mobile.

Matt introduced his best friend, "Hope you haven't been waiting long, this is my friend Alan Kawasaki."

"Friendly salutations," Alan offered. Matt gave him a look. Alan shrugged, unaware of what he did this time.

"Same to you," Allair replied. Allair's impression of Alan was that he was a nerd and an obvious virgin; Alan was a bit socially awkward.

Alan got into the back in order to make room for Allair. She got in the passenger side and everyone drove away.

A short while later, they pulled up to a storage unit. The unit's door was open and there was a Misfits-style horror/punk band practicing in full makeup.

"More of your unique friends?" Allair asked Matt.

"Yeah, we're just picking up Liz, Liz Ibelle., She's cool, you'll like her."

"Liz Ibelle? Like Jezebel?" Allair asked earnestly.

"Yeah, she's in a band," Alan chimed in from the back and continued with adding, "She's not bringing that grandiloquent gorilla with her, is she?"

"No, not Bruce, this time. After their last fight, she swears she's through with him for good, so we'll see." Matt turned to Allair to explain. "That's her boyfriend, and he's not coming. From the sounds of things, I think there's trouble in paradise."

Alan explained further by adding, "There is always drama with him, because he's so abusive. I don't know why she keeps going back."

Allair quickly jumped in, "I guess she must really love him. Sometimes when you care for someone, you do things you wouldn't normally do." Allair looked out the window, gripped her pants legs tightly in her fists, and wondered who she was truly talking about.

Liz Ibelle came storming out of the band practice. Liz Ibelle was slightly disturbed. She dressed in a Goth style. She gave off a vibe of a girl with a troubled past. She had been a cutter. She had gone through a traumatic life, and she really didn't give a fuck what anyone thought. She was covered in tattoos; they helped cover some scars on her body, but nothing hides the mental ones. She was known to go back to cutting in times of intense stress.

Behind Liz, a brutish-looking mass followed. He must be Bruce Mills. At his side, his boys followed in step; they could be considered his henchmen. They were logistically referred to by Bruce as his thugs. Bruce Mills believed you're not a man unless you've stepped inside the mixed martial arts cage. He was a real combat guy, always looking to show off the latest holds he'd learned. We all know a douche like him. He talked a lot of shit and was always looking for a fight. Bruce was also a liar and a manipulator. The thugs, One and Two, were constant sidekicks to Bruce. They had no discernable personalities of their own and were basically cloned copies of Bruce. They were Bruce's yes-men stooges.

Liz hollered, "I told you not to come here. I'm done with you and your fucking bullshit!"

Bruce grabbed Liz by the arm. "You don't know what you're talking about." He turned to the thugs, "Tell her how upset I was about last night..." Liz stopped fighting to get away from his grasp and turned her attention to hear the tale. She had an annoyed look on her face; this scenario had played out before.

Thug One was excited to offer help to the drama, "He was so upset, he showed up an hour late for the gym and you know how much he loves squats!" Thug Two jumped in next. "Out of everyone at the gym, he's got the strongest legs."

"They are like tree stumps," Thug One felt the need to help.

"Big round tree stumps," Thug Two finished.

Liz just stared at them and then exploded at their clone stupidity. "What the fuck are you talking about, you pathetic losers?"

Bruce spoke up, "Hey, don't talk to my boys like that! They wouldn't make me late to a workout."

"Well, maybe when they're done kissing your ass, you can spin around and let then suck your dick." Liz jibed. Bruce reeled back and punched Liz in the gut, causing her to double over. Bruce yelled, "Now look what you made me do. You know how I feel about all that homo shit. Fuck."

The car emptied, and Alan and Allair immediately attended to Liz while Matt headed in the direction where Bruce has stormed off. The thugs stayed behind and pushed Matt back. All Matt could do was holler after their leader. "Hey, Bruce, you can't do that man, Hey, Bruce!"

Seeing the pointlessness, Matt returned to Liz, and the thugs followed after Bruce.

"What kind of man hits a woman?" Allair looked at Matt shocked, "Is he a friend of yours?" Matt shook his head.

Liz yelled out to Bruce. "That's my EX-BOYFRIEND Bruce."

Allair consoled Liz for a moment as Alan took this scene all in.

Alan awkwardly approached Liz, "So, I ah, overheard that you're single now, thought maybe we could."

Matt hit Alan on the shoulder and gave him a horrified look. The girls went into the car, leaving the men alone. "What? Why'd you hit me," Alan asked as he rubbed out the soreness.

"Not now!" Matt said patiently to his socially inept friend. "Wait for the right time."

"It's been twenty-nine years. When's the right time?"

"Not after she takes a punch to the gut. Dammit, Alan, you'll know!"

Matt walked to the car. Alan stood alone and contemplative.

Alan exasperatedly threw his hands in the air, "Jesus..."

William Buck, the overly protective and religious older brother of Allair, would have never approved of her going off to a nudist resort.

Hell, typically he wouldn't have approved of her going to a fully clothed party. He believed in wholesomeness, purity, and righteousness, especially when all those values pertained to his sister. He sat, looking at the faces of an unfortunate family that listened to him. He was an unwelcomed guest in their home. He prattled on about his favorite religion. The mother and father looked for an opening to get rid of him while an impressionable young lady sat wide-eyed listening.

"Christ loves you, and you, and especially you! I have a cupcake for you, and it has a cross on it! Just like the cross that our Lord and Savior died painfully on for our sins. He was so bloody and beaten, nails driven into his flesh, as the hot sun burned down upon his Jewish head. A crown of thorns dug deep into his skull."

The family looked at each other in horror.

Unaware of their uncomfortableness, he continued, "I always say salvation tastes better with sprinkles." He placed some tracts down next to the cupcake and happily waved and smiled as he strutted out the door and on toward the next family he would attempt to convert. The family was left in shock. William walked to a park and sat on a bench and dial his sister.

Inside the college dorm room, the phone rang.

Emily answered, "Hello?"

"Why, hello, Emily! How are you on this fine day which the Lord has blessed us all with?"

"I'm fine." Not wanting to chitchat with this Bible-beater, she quickly added, "Allair is not here."

"Oh, do you know when my dear sister might be back?"

"Oh, she's gone all weekend."

"Went on some kind of Bible retreat, did she? A 'lil missionary trip; that always makes me feel..."

"Well, I don't know about the missionary position, but she will be naked." Emily was irritated and loved making this guy uncomfortable.

William was stunned. NOT HIS SWEET SISTER. She was being corrupted.

Emily got in a fatal blow by stating, "She left with her boyfriend for a bit of nudist camping."

William dropped the phone and looked up, praying.

Emily's voice rang out from the dropped phone. "Hello...? Hello? You still there?"

After a moment, William picked up the phone and gasped out, "Camping? Nude? Boyfriend? Missionary?"

Emily smiled slyly, "It does sound fun when you put it like that, doesn't it?"

"No, no, it doesn't, not at all. Emily! That's my sister! I'm coming over right now!"

Emily gulped, "Okay."

Deep in the woods the TV sat nearby a cabin. The messed-up fellow sat in a chair and sharpened a knife. The TV played the familiar static.

Matt, Allair, and company drove into the nudist resort check-in area. As they exited the car, Allair couldn't help but notice various naked bodies walking by with towels and flip-flops. Her anxiety continued to rise. At the front desk, the group was greeted by a fully nude older man in his 60s, who moments earlier was putting away various science lab coats. One of the coats had a badge that named Dr. Chambers as its owner. On the wall, a painted print of Edouard Manet's "Luncheon on the Grass." was displayed. There was also a framed photo of Ms. Fraga, the art instructor from Miskatonic University next to the notice of that day's lunch special: Nudist Salad, came with no dressing. The older gentleman was the caretaker of the Bare Bear Nudist Resort. His eyes gave the impression that he might know more than he let on. He was a friendly but slightly odd fellow.

Matt whispered to Allair, "Remember, eye contact."

Liz ran over to the caretaker and gave him a big naked hug. They always looked forward to seeing each other. "Are those science researchers still here, Teddy?"

"Nope. Left earlier; science folks have always been interested in the outer woods around here for as long as I can remember." Then Teddy quickly moved on; he chose to change the subject. Addressing Liz, he asked, "Are you still seeing that Bruce character?"

"No! We broke up today, this time for good. I mean it." Liz replied.

"You should have seen him hit her; it was brutal." Liz and Teddy looked at Alan.

"It's a good thing he left; I was going to have to do something." Teddy let out a patient breath.

"Well, I'm happy for you. You deserve a good man in your life." Teddy slapped Alan on the back, and he gave him a knowing look. Alan previously shared how he felt about Liz with Teddy. The various greetings continued all around the friends.

Teddy then addressed the unfamiliar face, "Who's your new friend?"

"Oh, this is Allair Buck. She's a student at Miskotonic. It's okay, she's with me. She's a textile, or at least for a little longer." Matt and Allair exchanged glances.

Allair motioned to the reproduced painting by Manet. "Art for Art's sake. You know that was the beginning of a whole new wave where the artists didn't need a backstory to explain what they put out in the world. Before that, it was all clamshells and wheat fields."

"Or Dante's inferno," Teddy chuckled. "I've heard some great things about you, Allair." Matt gave him a *shut-up* look. Teddy continued ignoring him. "So, are you looking forward to the karaoke party and dance on Saturday? Assume that's what you're up here for."

Allair forced out, "I sure am. Sounds like a lot of fun." Allair tried to make it sound believable.

"I know Alan is looking forward to it. Hey, your 'ol buddy Jambalaya Jefferson is working tonight. When he gets off maybe you two can get a chess game in or go look at the stars," Teddy sounded excited.

"Oh, I haven't seen him since the eclipse, the night we had that body painting contest." Alan laughed and smiled as he interjected.

"I still think I should have won that body-painting contest." Liz muttered as they left on their way to naked adventures.

The group was fully nude at the swimming pool area, all except for Allair who had a white towel wrapped around her. They eagerly made their way to the pool area where various other nudists were enjoying the day.

Alan announces triumphantly, "We're finally naked! God! I never thought we'd get naked."

They started jumping into the pool. All around pleasant scenes of fun played out; there was a lot of splashing around with various body types. Allair took off her towel, revealing her very conservative one-piece bathing suit. She looked at the fully nude body of Matt, who looked completely comfortable.

Matt gently informed Allair, "It's not allowed for anyone to be in the water with a suit on. It's a clothes fibers thing, clogs the filter."

Allair looked at him like he was lying, "Yeah, right. Okay."

Matt's face didn't give any indication that he was kidding, "It's only clothing optional outside of pool and hot tub areas. Really."

She nodded at Matt and took a seat on a pool-side recliner. Alan floated over to her side of the pool. She struck up a conversation, "So, have you always been a nudist, naturist, naked guy? What do I call you?"

"Call me Alan. There's all different kinds of us, and it doesn't matter what you call us. Look around." Allair looked around. "There are nudists, naturists, artists, exhibitionists, and, okay, even a few awkward weirdos like me. But we're harmless. My first time here, I was a voyeur. I came to see the girls, but then I discovered that there was a sense of family. I was finally comfortable in my own skin for the first time ever. I'd never had that feeling before. Maybe you don't quite understand?"

"No, I totally get it." Allair tried to sound comfortable.

Liz yelled over, "Are you getting all sappy again?" Then Liz addressed Allair. "Besides, way back when he wasn't a voyeur. He was a total perv." Liz splashed Alan with water. He took it in the face and attacked back, moving to her side of the pool.

Matt noticed four hippies enjoying the water and sun. Two of the naturalists were friends of Matt. He waved to his buddies.

Geoff & Summer were two happy, hairy hippies in a long-term loving relationship. Both of them have dreadlocks, and both look like they just got back from "Burning Man." They embodied the Zen, yoga, pot, and peace 'n love lifestyle. They were joined by Bob and Marley, a patchouli-smelling couple. He had a Rastafarian hat on, and she had an oversized tie-dye t-shirt accessorized by a hemp over-the-shoulder bag.

Geoff & Summer wished Matt and his friends well and made plans to meet up later. They said in unison, "See you later."

Matt was rubbing suntan lotion on Allair's shoulders and neck. Matt whispered, "Relax, you'll come to love it here. It's the safest place on Earth." Allair looked up at him. She did love him, even if he's kind of unique fellow.

Bob was thrown against a tree. He had been worked over pretty good, including having his eye torn out. He was strangely able to still be wearing the Rastafarian hat. Marley had the back of her T-shirt torn open, exposing the scratches on her back from the long-fingered alien. She still clutched the hemp bag as she ran to her fallen mate. Just then an inhuman looking stick figure appears. Marley tried waking the barely living Bob. Her pierced nipples grazed his bare skin. Her fear was focused on the body of sticks when the long, Cthulhu-like noodle arms of a second alien came from around the back of the tree. She didn't notice at first when it grabbed hold of Bob's ears and began to tear at his flesh. She noticed too late as his face was torn in two, leaving muscle tissue and skull.

Marley screamed and ran away, attempting to escape. She ran directly into the stick bodied alien and fell backwards with her bag falling off of her. The stick was tall and towered above her. Between its legs, a smaller, cute little alien appeared. The ball of fluff with large innocent looking eyes looked up at Marley for a moment. Marley felt she might be spared. The small bubble shaped alien began poking Marley's hemp bag that had fallen to the ground, and it began to glow. In an attempt to communicate, Marley picked up her bag and waved it around. The bubble alien freaked out and backed away. The noodle-armed alien wrapped its tentacles around Marley's feet and began to drag her. The purse continued to glow. Sticks grabbed her arms and pulled her back. A slight tug-of-war began that completely ripped her in half.

Marley cried out for the last time, "Oh god, please... JESUS!"

William stood with Emily and attempted to get more information from her. "The Lord is the only man she should be focused on right now. Tell me again about this Matt, and why can't he keep his pants on?"

Emily was tired of talking with him. "You're such a knob jockey sometimes. She's an adult, William. I can't believe you don't trust your sister to make the right decision."

"I trust her; I just don't trust Matt and his friend, Lucifer! I'll tell you what we're going to do. We are going to this den of devils and we are going to get back MY SISTER!"

"We? What do you mean us?" Emily stepped back from William.

"If you don't show me where this place is, then I won't help you with your problem." They looked at each other for a moment.

Emily finally sighed, "Fine, let's fucking go."

Matt sat next to Allair, while Summer and Geoff splashed in the water and talked with Alan and Liz.

Geoff turned toward Matt, "So, where are you all crashing tonight?"

Matt responded, "We brought camping gear and were going to camp out by the volleyball net."

"You all should join Summer and I. We are sleeping at that haunted cabin!" Geoff would make spooky sounds and tease Summer about it. Liz was very interested. This was right up her alley.

Liz asked, "Did you say its haunted?"

"Yeah, there's some story." Matt added.

"The possibility of a poltergeist or apparition at a nudist resort cabin is more than highly unlikely." said Alan, the eternal buzz kill.

Liz ignored the negativity and said, "I think it sounds fucking badass. I'm in!"

Alan changed his mind suddenly, "I didn't say I wouldn't go. I mean, I really should investigate, you know... in the name of science. Plus, then..." Alan motioned to Matt, thinking that he may have finally made the right move. "Your girl can enjoy the private hot tub later in the comfort of her one-piece 1920s bathing suit and shower cap. Hey, Allair. Where's your shower cap?"

"Why are you all teasing?" Allair looked around to see she was still the only one clothed. "Oh, I don't mind getting unclothed."

"Yes, we can all see that." Liz said.

Allair got up to go. "Okay, let's get going to that cabin."

They all got ready to hustle off. Before they got very far, an older black man spoke up while mopping the floor. Jambalaya Jefferson was a fixture at the Bare Bear, "If I were you, I'd steer clear of that cabin. Bad things happen up there. People go missin' and such. One night, I saw these strange lights, and these bubbles..."

Teddy walked through, "Y'all pay Jambalaya no mind now, kids. You go have fun, but whatever you do, stay naked. Damn fool kids today can't keep their clothes off."

"You got it T, like that's ever going to be a problem with me!?" Liz strutted her naked, scarred and tatted up body by him. Teddy noticed Allair still wearing the one-piece. "This goes for the new girl too. Allair, while you're here I need you to follow the rules. Taking off your clothes..." He paused to choose the right words. "It's for your very own safety."

Allair thought to herself, *sheesh they take that fiber clogging thing seriously*. "No problem Teddy, it's taken care of," Allair quietly replied.

"Yeah," Alan adds. "We are making progress. Look, she already took off her shower cap!"

Allair just went with it, "Yeah, hey, does this mean I'm topless?" She pointed to her head. "Look at me, I'm topless over here."

Liz shook her head. "Yeah, she's a real risk-taker over here."

They walked off onto a trail; Summer and Geoff led the way. Once the group was out of sight, Jambalaya looked at Teddy, he saw that Teddy was disappointed in him. Jambalaya Jefferson lowered his head and continued to mop; he mumbled about those damn kids. As Teddy turned to leave the pool area, he ran into Bruce and his cohorts, the thugs, all fully dressed.

"Bruce, you are over-dressed for tonight. What are you doing here?" Teddy was irritated with the bully.

"Teddy, I'm looking for Liz. Have you seen her around here?"

"I saw her, says she broke up with you for good. Can't say's I blame her with the way you always treat her." He looked over at Jambalaya. "What is it with the name Bruce, anyway? Bruces are always assholes! I'm serious, I've never met a cool Bruce."

Thug One laughed. Bruce was shocked that his lackeys would dare laugh at his expense. "Hey, shut up, Thugs!" Thug One and Thug Two lowered their heads in shame. Bruce felt the need to address Teddy again, "Listen up, old man. If you don't want me to pound your one hundred-year-old ass into the ground, you'll tell me where she is."

Teddy thought a moment. *Can he do this? Should he do this? He will do it.* He looked at Bruce and the thugs. "Okay. Yes, I've seen her. She's at the haunted cabin. That way." Teddy pointed toward the trail. They began to leave. "But, Bruce, guys, folks can see you on the trail from the road, so I'm going to ask that you keep your clothes on, okay?"

"Yeah, that's not a problem." Bruce paused for a moment of sincerity, "Teddy, I know you care about Liz. I care about her too."

"I'm sure you do." He yelled after him. "Don't forget to keep your clothes on."

Once they left, Ol' Jambalaya looked over at Teddy and just shook his head.

Inside the spooky lone cabin, the screen of the television was smashed. A lone figure exited the room and slammed the door.

The nude group included Liz, Alan, Summer, Geoff, and Matt. Everyone was nude except Allair. They walked along the trail in the wilderness. They reached a clearing and Liz moved off to the side. "Hey, guys, can you hold up?" She huffed and held her side.

"Is this because you used to smoke a pack a day? I'm so happy you've cut back on those. Maybe you still have plaque buildup in your lungs." Alan looked at her sweetly, like a dumb puppy. Liz was annoyed with him.

Allair came to her aid, "Or maybe it's because she was punched in the stomach earlier? Geez." Both girls, Summer & Allair, comforted Liz by complaining about the troubles with men. Alan moved closer to Matt. He felt outnumbered by the estrogen levels.

"I always say the wrong thing." Alan said to Matt, clearly disappointed. Matt patted Alan on the back as he walked by. Matt talked with Geoff, and Alan explored the rock formations nearby.

"So, what do you think of Allair?" Matt asked, "She's sweet, right?" They both turned to look at her. She and Summer were tending to Liz. They were having some girl time.

Geoff answered, "I'm happy for you, seems like you found a good one. Now when's she gonna get naked?" They both chuckled.

Alan held up what he had just found. "Wasn't this Marley's shirt from earlier?" Alan had a torn tie-dyed shirt in his hand.

"Oh, cool!" Summer said, "They must be around here."

Geoff took a rolled joint out from behind his ear and held it proudly in the glistening sunlight. "You guys go on to the cabin without us. We're gonna hang out on this STONE and get STONED!"

"Oh, my gawd" Summer giggled. "Did you just say that!?" Geoff and Summer had a loving embrace as the others half rolled their eyes and began to leave them be.

Alan dropped the torn tie-died shirt on the rock.

After much smoking, Summer and Geoff laughed while lying on the large, flat rock. Summer had the colorful torn shirt in her hand.

"Something tells me she won't need this anymore!" Summer said as she tossed the shirt behind her.

The shirt flew through the air in an arc and unnoticed by the couple it is caught quickly and silently by an alien claw that appeared suddenly at the last moment before the shirt hit the ground. The fabric of the shirt glowed in the claw in the eyes of the creature while all other shapes faded in the background. The rustling of footsteps broke the silence, and the alien turned from Summer and Geoff to see three glowing outfits of clothing coming their way.

It was the oblivious Bruce and his thugs. Teddy had suggested they keep their clothes on, and strangely they obeyed.

"What a surprise, never would have guessed you two would be here getting high," Bruce announced to Geoff.

"You should try it. It mellows you out, man."

Bruce flexed and said, "There's no time to be mellow when you're in the cage."

"There's nothing cool about hurting someone," said Summer. "Besides, I don't support the suffering of another human being."

Bruce was getting angry and directed it at Geoff for not keeping his woman in line and for being an overall failure. He directed him in a life lesson. "Look, I'm not addressing the female, but you're not a man unless you step in the cage against another man. There's no third place. There's no place. There's one winner, with one hand raised, and when you're in the cage with me, it's my hand because I'm the winner. The only true champion; you got that?"

"Yeah, he's the champ!" The thugs hooted and hollered. "Bruce is the man, he's undefeated."

Summer and Geoff said in unison, "Wow."

Bubbles started to appear from near the rock where Summer and Geoff were lying. Bubbles popped all around them, and everyone was truly entertained by this. Summer turned to Geoff and whispered, "This is really good weed."

The bubbles had a numbing effect on the minds of the naked Summer and Geoff. They were on a really good trip. There were colors, swirls, and LSD/PCP-a kind of crazy loony fun going on. One of the bubbles got closer to Bruce and the thugs. The fuzzy little alien climbed up on the rock. The little thing sat between Summer and Geoff. They were happy to see it. It was like it might grant them wishes or something. The fuzzy creature cuddled up with Summer, who happily pet it. "I think I will call this cute thing Bubbles." Meanwhile the other men started to trip out. The surrounding area began to swirl, and they saw shapes coming in from the night. Noodle-arms stepped out from the darkness and caught Thug One's attention. "What the..."

Suddenly, the noodle-arm creature was right in front of him. Its gaping mouth and fangs were seen briefly in this drug-induced scene.

Thug One breathed, "...hell!"

The thug turned to the other thug and tried to get his attention; he was obviously very out of it. He raised a bloody stub and dazedly asked, "Didn't I used to have a hand?" The appendage exposed his bone and spurted a light fountain of blood. The open fanged mouth was bloodier than before.

Thug Two turned to answer him in this drug induced bubbly haze, "What?"

As he turned to talk, his right ear and the side of his face had been torn away in a horrific display that freaked out Bruce. Bruce was so freaked out by this nightmare that he turned to run. He left his thugs behind and ran. He ran for what felt like forever, and then he ran into a wall. The impact knocked him backward, and he landed next to his thugs! All the running got him nowhere. He'd run in a circle. His thugs were screaming and pleading to live. One's head was in the mouth of Noodle Arms and was being chewed on. Two's stomach was torn open, and his intestines were being pulled out in an evil scene. Bruce looked up at the wall that he ran into as the drug bubbles began to trip him back out. The wall appeared to be another demon creature to him. This alien appeared to be more of a warrior alien. Warrior was really big. He looked like a barbaric Viking. He had spikes coming off his shoulders like the WWE Tag Team, Legion of Doom, Road Warriors. He was clearly a brute fighter. Bruce saw this new creature through his warped drug haze. He rose to fight! *Enough running, damn it*; Bruce was a fighter, and he was going to back it up. He got in the face of Warrior, and through his blurred vision he saw three aliens. Bruce got multiple punches in at Warriors chest. These punches bloodied up his fists, but they did not phase Warrior at all. He backed off a moment and then came in with a big right hook. Warrior then pulled Bruce's right hand up to catch the forearm, and his left arm smacked below the elbow. Bruce's arm was broken. Bruce's left hand slid down to the crook of the elbow, and there was another snap. His left arm was pulled down into the crook in order to put him off balance, and Warrior's right hand came into Bruce's right eye., In one swift movement, Warrior took the eyeball out as his left arm brought Bruce's body down, revealing he had taken his eye. Bruce laid in a crumpled heap with a broken arm, missing eye, bloodied knuckles, and an overall broken spirit. Warrior examined the eyeball while Bruce crawled off in the background. Warrior looked at it closely and then tossed it towards Summer and Geoff on the rock. After it landed near them, Bubbles reached for it. Summer and Geoff were still having the time of their lives. Summer thought the eye was a flower; she thought it was a beautiful sunflower, with an eyeball in the middle. Bubbles put the severed eye between Summer's pierced breasts, so it resembled a middle nipple. Summer looked at it happily; she believed it was a nice ornament. It blinked at her. They were all having a great time. They fell into the pools of blood and began making *blood angels*.

Back at the cabin, the group heard some spooky noises, and they sounded like they were going after Liz.

Liz was yelling, "Alan... Alan, I'm a... not a scared of you."

Liz settled and stood still, listening intently, "Boo!" Alan jumped out, and Liz fell back, tripping over a box. "You're an asshole!"

Alan felt bad and asked, "Do you need help to get up?"

Liz slapped Alan's extended hand, "I can do it, you helped enough. I don't know how you can be the smartest man I've ever known, but also the dumbest?"

"So, I'm your everything," Alan beamed.

"Your mind is so amazing. You know so many things that I couldn't imagine knowing, but then outta nowhere you'll do something so ridiculously stupid." She sighed. "Maybe that's why I'm so fascinated by you."

Alan was surprised. This was news to him, "You are, really?"

"That's what makes you such a good *friend*." Liz replied. That was not what he wanted to hear.

Meanwhile, Matt turned on the hot tub, and the bubbles were going.

"It's nice out here," Allair purred. "It's a great night for some hot tubbing." Allair put her leg up on the hot tub and stretched. "That hike really wore me out. I can't wait to get in this tub and loosen my muscles."

"It shouldn't take too long to warm up." Matt stretched out as well.

"It's nice just being here with you."

"I feel the same way." Matt held Allair in an embrace. "It wasn't too bad, right? Not too many... what'd you call 'em, crazy pervert freak shows walking around?"

"Nope," She paused a moment before continuing, "You're the only one."

Liz sat on a bed while Alan was going through the box she stumbled over earlier. "Have you found anything interesting in there?"

"Yeah, all this stuff is fascinating,"

Liz was intrigued, "Really, what is it?"

"Looks like paperwork from those scientists that Matt was talking about. They must have left it behind." While going through the papers he continued, "Says here they found technetium."

"Is he a rapper? I didn't know he was missing." Alan was bothered by her lack of intellect. Why was he always surrounded by dumb people?

"Technetium is the element with atomic number forty-three. As everyone knows it's the lowest atomic number without any isotopes, so every form of it is radioactive. Almost all Technetium is produced synthetically."

"So are most of my orgasms. What's your point, science boy?"

"These papers say that they found an abundance of it here in these woods. Naturally, well, that isn't even possible." Alan sat back in contemplation.

"So? Maybe they were wrong. What's the big fucking deal?"

Alan ran his hand through his hair, "The big deal is this, if they weren't wrong, this is a huge break. Whoever wrote these notes found something in these woods that is not of this Earth."

"Well, if it's in the woods on Earth, then it's of Earth, right? Either that or they found some of Geoff and Summer's weed! That stuff is radioactive." Liz chuckled at her own joke.

Alan wondered why he even tried, "It's a good thing you're pretty."

"Huh?"

Alan muttered, "Never mind."

Liz looked out the window. "They sure do look pretty cute together."

Matt and Allair were both in the bubbles enjoying the heated flowing water. They were enjoying a quiet, peaceful moment. They were unaware that they were watched from the woods.

Matt leaned in to Allair, "Know what this moment needs?"

"What's that?"

Matt smiled, "Some wine."

"Wait, huge moment for us and our relationship, red wine or white wine?" She looked semiserious.

"White. Sweet wine, of course."

"If you'd said red wine, I was going to leave right now; it gives me a headache."

"Woman after my heart, I'll be right back." Matt jumped out of the tub and noticed the towel on his side of the tub. He tossed it to Allair. "You might need this." It hit her playfully. She put it on her side as he went in the cabin door. She dunked her head under the bubbles and when she came back up the towel was gone. A glimpse of it being lost into the darkness of the night, unnoticed by Allair. She stood up and was kinda freaked out. Matt, Liz, and Alan all came storming back out.

"Are you okay? I thought I saw someone out here just now," Matt yelled.

Allair was confused and looked around, "They took my towel?"

Liz sniffed the air, "What's that smell? It smells like garbage."

"You all go in the cabin. I'm going to see who this peeping tom is." Matt grabbed a flashlight and stormed off to investigate. Allair went inside with Liz and Alan.

Allair, Liz, and Alan stood looking out the window. Matt was in the woods, looking around with a flashlight. He heard a rustling noise from behind him and he turned around. "I know you're out there! You are not allowed to be here if you're not a member."

Out of the darkness, he heard more rustling. "This isn't a peep show."

The rustling stopped. All was quiet for just a moment. Then suddenly, as Matt turned to his right, a flashlight beam fell on the twisted, contorted face of a bloody hippy. Summer's face was frozen in shock, and she screamed, "Ahhhhhhhhhhhh!"

Geoff suddenly appeared out from behind, "Dead, all dead man; dead, dead, dead…"

Matt started getting nervous, "Calm down guys, I think you had a bad trip. Let's get you back to the cabin and relax." He noticed that they were covered in a dark brownish-red liquid. "And, let's wash all that paint off."

Matt along with the shocked and bloodied hippy couple exploded into the cabin with Summer as she ranted.

"Calm down, calm down…" Matt said., He turned to Allair, Liz, and Alan, "They are having a bad trip. This is why I don't do drugs."

Allair was much more concerned, "Oh, my god, are they going to be ok?"

Matt offered, "Yeah, we just need to wash the paint off them."

"I miss mushrooms," Liz said to Summer, who had quieted down and was staring into space. "Wow, what do you see?"

"Listen, I'm not fucking around," Geoff pled. "There are bodies out there. Look at me. I'm covered in their blood."

"Yeah, a regular maxi pad. How come nobody told me you had mushrooms," Liz asked

"Well, you didn't ask," Geoff responded. "You need to listen, there were bubbles and colors, furry little critters, it was the greatest feeling of my life."

Everyone listened, their eyes darting back and forth at each other. This druggy lived some life. "Then there were arms, and legs, and eyeballs, insides, and blood. So much blood. It was Bruce Mills and his two thugs. Torn to pieces."

Liz listened now, "Bruce? You saw Bruce? I don't like this story."

Allair then tried to sound casual, "Well, I don't like how they took my towel."

Matt consoled the girls, "It's okay girls, and he's just talking nonsense."

"This is real, I'm not…" Geoff took this moment to vomit a lot. He threw up more than he had before in his life, or perhaps anyone ever has before on record. Yes, that's a lot of puke.

Allair held it together long enough to guide him off to the restroom while he continued to spray. Summer sat; she was still comatose and rocked in the corner as Liz talked with Matt and Alan.

"On second thought, I don't want those 'shrooms." Liz looked at Summer. "Hey, did you two really see Bruce?"

Summer rocked back and forth, creeping out Liz. Summer kept mumbling, "Bub-bles…"

Suddenly the eerie silence was broken; a scream rang out from the bathroom and caught everyone's attention. They ran into the bathroom. Liz Ibelle, Alan Kawasaki, Allair, Buck, Matt Stanton, and Summer saw Geoff passed out beside the toilet, and Allair freaked out. On top of the pungent vomit, in the toilet, sat a severed eyeball. Allair's innocent eyes observed a human being throw up an eyeball.

"What is that!?" Allair hugged Matt's chest. "What is that?"

"Let me save you the scientific jargon," Alan said. "It appears to be a human eyeball."

Liz said, "What color is it?" Not wanting to look herself.

"It's probably puke green." Alan said quickly.

"Damn it, Alan, I'm serious. I want to know if it's Bruce's," Liz stuttered.

"Let's just assume it is and all celebrate. What do you think? Geoff and Summer went on a cannibalistic rampage and had a craving for macho insecurities and suppressed homosexuality?"

Liz slammed Alan against the wall, "What's the fucking eye color?"

Alan stumbled to his knees in the human waste slop and announced, "It's brown." That was not what she wanted to hear. Her fears were confirmed; it could be her former boyfriend.

Liz approached Matt, "I need to know if he's out there."

Alan, still on his knees, said, "Only an idiot would go out now. We got two people covered in what might be blood, one spitting up human body parts..."

Liz was serious, she needed answers.

Matt cut Alan off, "If you go out there Liz, you can't just wander out in the woods by yourself?"

"We could see if he pukes up any more of him." Alan looked at the faces of his friends, who were not amused. "What?"

Liz saw that Matt and Allair were together. Summer and Geoff were in shock or passed out. Liz looked at the only remaining soul, Alan. "Just for that, you are going with me."

Summer woke up momentarily. "...We were making angels in the pretty red snow..." She then rocked herself slowly; she was lost in her own world.

A long claw hand picked up fabric from the thugs. There were various body parts strewn about. Sticks was doing its duty. He carried a bag made from dried human skin. Alan and Liz watched from the bushes. They would never forget what they had seen.

Liz held Alan's shoulder close and whispered to him, "Do you think that thing has Bruce?"

"Shh... We're watching it, but maybe they're also watching us?" There were moments of quiet.

Liz broke the silence, "We have to follow where it goes."

"Quiet... please." Alan was freaked out and looked over his shoulders, side to side. The creature began its trek back to where it came from.

"I'm going to go follow it." Liz got up.

Alan whispered, "No..."

"Come with me or stay here by yourself."

"Yup I'll be here, safely all by myself, alive all by myself." He reluctantly looked at her and continued through clenched teeth, "Okay, I'll go. This isn't a good idea."

Liz saw that he was scared. She knew he always liked her more than she likes him, so she gave him a quick peck on the lips. He felt invigorated and was overjoyed; perhaps this was the greatest moment of his life.

Liz said, "Thank you."

They got up and followed Sticks. A moment later there was rustling in the bushes. Somebody or something was watching them. Just then a very injured Bruce stumbled out from the darkness. His eye socket was empty, and his arm was damaged. He had been hiding in the woods for hours. He was not happy, and he was not a happy man to begin with. He saw Liz kiss Alan.

"Fucking nerd," Bruce hobbled off after them.

Geoff felt better, but he still felt sick. He focused on Summer, who looked lost in another world. Matt attempted to reassure everyone. "I'm sure they'll come back with great news. Let us know that it's all a misunderstanding. You both took some powerful drugs. We've all been there." He looked at Allair, who clearly had never taken drugs before.

"I don't know, man. That was so realistic." Geoff put his head in his hands. "We woke up surrounded by bodies."

"No, you didn't." Allair rubbed his back.

"You were probably still coming down off of it. It was laced or something. I'm just glad you both made it to me and didn't run into Teddy; you know how he feels about people doing drugs at the resort..." Matt thought about it a second, and then added with a chuckle, "Without offering him any."

Geoff took a deep breath, "Yeah, you're right. It was so wild."

"I bet it was," Allair said. Summer looked at them as if to ask if it was all real.

"I haven't had such a bad trip since Burning Man 2006," Geoff offered to Summer. "Now that was a year."

Summer looked at them more clearly now. "I remember Burning Man..." She smiled.

Alan and Liz watched as Sticks carried his sack and entered a sort of portal. He just stepped through a tree. Sticks never looked behind itself, and just pressed through.

"Okay, it's gone, there's nothing left to follow! We know where it came from." Alan said. Liz was conflicted about leaving just yet. Alan turned to leave, "Let's go back and warn the others." Just then Alan ran into Bruce, who pushed him backward.

Liz was shocked, "What the hell happened to you?"

"Shut up bitch, this is your fucking fault. First, I came out here and get my ass beat by a reptile that doesn't fight by the state athletic commission's official guidelines, and then I see you locking lips with nerd-boy 'Adam' over here."

Alan offered the correct pronunciation of his name, "Alan." Bruce kicked him in the stomach.

"My name's Bruce, faggot," Bruce turned from a crumpled Alan to face Liz. "And as for you..." He raised his hand as if to hit her. She winced. "I'll deal with you later after we fix my fucking face. Here's what we're gonna do. First, I'm going to..." He was suddenly cut off by a hit from behind; a large piece of wood took him off balance and made him fall forward.

Alan had enough of all this, and he stood proudly behind him. Bruce was momentarily quiet.

"You're not going to touch her anymore," Alan proclaimed. Bruce was a little impressed that Alan finally stepped into the cage. Alan continued to tell Bruce off, "You were never good enough for her. She is the most beautiful woman in the world, and you've kept her black and blue. Does that make you a man? That doesn't make you a man. You are a boy stuck in a big ass body."

Bruce stood up and looked at Liz. She was visibly impressed. Bruce was going to kill Alan. Bruce said to Liz, "Look who has a crush. Well, I'm going to crush his head."

Just as Bruce went for Alan something grabbed him from behind and pulled him backward. He landed on his back, and the warrior alien stomped on Bruce's chest. Warrior then stared right at Liz and Alan. He saw right through Liz and Alan; he sniffed and knew that there was somebody there, but it was not an enemy. Liz and Alan weren't sure what to do, so they just watched as it brought a whistle up to its monster mouth and blew.

The portal behind Liz and Alan burped with Sticks; and he crossed over with a bag to collect yet again. He walked right between Liz and Alan, not *seeing* them.

Alan whispered, "They don't see us."

Sticks moved toward Bruce, who was still alive, barely. The long creature tore at his skin and flesh in an attempt to retrieve the clothing.

Bruce hollered between his last screams. "Fuck you Adam." Bits of clothing and hunks of his bloody organs are tossed about.

"No, fuck you Bruce, Fuck you." Alan pulled Liz towards himself.

She turned away, burying her face in his shoulder. Alan felt great as they embraced.

Alan started talking, "It's the clothes, they want the clothes. That story we heard earlier. It's not the ghosts, but it is something else." He turned from his thoughts to the woman in his arms. There was sudden silence. All was quiet while horror was going on behind them. There were bits flying through the air, yet all they saw was each other. Liz saw Alan for the first time. They locked eyes, and they kissed; it was really good. Alan's eyes opened and closed as they kissed, and he noticed a bit of clothing float down towards Liz; it almost looked like a snowflake. A larger bit of fabric got closer, and on one of his last blinks he ssuddenaw that the fabric fell onto her shoulder. In a split second a claw grabbed her shoulder, pulling into a vicious mauling. Instantly, she was gone, gone forever, his lost love. Alan got splashed in his face with Liz's blood.

Allair, Summer, Matt, and Geoff dealt with calming things back down.

"I'm glad you are all feeling better," Allair said.

"It all seemed so real," Summer said.

"Yeah, I agree with Summer," Geoff said. "Where the hell did that Halloween eyeball come from? So weird, most realistic trip I've ever been on."

"You can say that again."

"You don't want to do that again. You scared all of us," Matt said.

"I was freaked out when I saw the eyeball," Allair said. "Looked so real..."

"Sorry to scare you all. I still feel like I need to sleep this off." Summer cuddled into Geoff, agreeing with what he said with her body.

"Maybe we should go for a walk; get some fresh air and leave these two alone?" Allair smiled at Matt. "Sounds nice, no more excitement for tonight. Besides, we don't want to keep you two up with our talking and stuff." Matt stood up and took Allair by the hand. Allair stood along with Matt, and they turned towards the door.

"See you two in a little while." Matt and Allair left the former mental patients. They began their walk towards the woods.

"Suppose this is more action than you were expecting." Matt held Allair's hand.

"For sure," they both laughed. They belonged together.

"I promise from here on out it'll be smooth sailing; nothing but peace and relaxation."

"I was right about you. I'm not sure I'm ready to take my clothes off yet in a social setting like this, but when I do, I want you there." Matt and Allair looked longingly into each other's eyes.

"Oh hey, I have to show you something." He grabbed her hand, and they raced off towards the wilderness.

Geoff and Summer cuddled together; they were warm under blankets. All is quiet and peaceful at last. The night sky was visible from their window, and the earlier horror seemed to be all a dream.

Matt and Allair made their way through the brush and toward a hidden beach. Once there, they started to go into the water and Allair stopped. She took his hand, and he turned to look at her. She slowly took off her swimsuit. Matt noticed her hesitation, and that she was scared. She felt vulnerable. He stopped her just as the straps barely left her shoulders. He pulled them back up.

"We can wait." She loved this naked man. He understood her. She understood that this was not some crazy sex fetish, but being a nudist is truly nonsexual acceptance of herself. They kissed. Afterward, they began to splash around and play like kids in the water under the moon.

Matt and Allair made their way back towards the cabin. Love was in the air. All was right with the world. Geoff and Summer cuddled into each other at the cabin; they enjoyed some REM sleep.

Summer talked in her sleep, "Who's a cute pink puppy, you are. Yes, you are." The night wind rolled outside. All was right with the world until… BOOM! Suddenly, the cabin door flew open, and Alan stood in the doorway. He was covered with blood, and his eyes were wide with shock.

"They killed Liz." The hippie population awoke startled. Alan continued ranting and rambling to himself as he looked around. "Where's Matt & Allair? We need to get out of here. They killed Liz. Oh, no you don't." He grabbed the blankets off them. "Fabric will get you killed. Trust me. All linens are bad."

Geoff was still half asleep, "What about John Linen? Everyone likes the Beatles…"

Summer turned to Geoff, "Are we tripping again?"

Geoff was awake now and not happy, "What's going on?"

Through the open-door William Buck arrived followed by Emily.

He started, "That's what I'd like to know. What in the name of our Heavenly Father is going on around here?"

Alan is aghast that they were still wearing clothes under the circumstances, "Quick, take your clothes off, now."

Noodle-arms oozed in thru an open window unnoticed by everyone else.

"Get away from me, you unholy freak. What is that on you? Blood, have you godless pagans been sacrificing small animals? Where's my sister? I swear she better not be naked…" William was still reeling.

Alan turned away like in a bad soap opera, "If she's not naked, she's probably dead by now…" He dramatically turned back. "You need to bare all, both of you!"

"Oh, kinky." Emily said.

"Listen up pervert; no one gets William Buck naked."

Noodle-Arms let out a shriek and waved his jelly arms. William and Emily turned to run in the opposite direction. Alan comforted Summer and Geoff quickly realizing that being naked meant that they were okay.

Alan held a finger up to his mouth, "Shhh, you're okay, trust me." The terrified Summer and Geoff looked at calm Alan. Had he figured something out? They looked back at where Noodle Arms was and saw only an open window. Bubbles started to come through the open window. Summer and Geoff screamed to close the window. Alan closed it hard.

William and Emily had run away from whatever it was they saw. William ran into the chest of Warrior alien. Warrior felt up, and those hands sank deep into his flesh. Almost too easily, Warrior came back up with his rib cage, and the blood was everywhere. Emily was freaked out beyond words. Sticks appeared behind Warrior and it lunged for her. She screamed and ran back to the now closed door of the cabin.

Emily hollered and slammed her fists on the door, "Please let me in. Open the bloody door." The three of them huddled behind the door.

"Take your clothes off," Alan yelled. "They want your clothes."

Emily looked at Sticks and watched William dying on the ground. She immediately disrobed as Sticks got closer to her. When she was completely nude, the door opened, and she was pulled to safety just as Sticks' claws reached for the clothes she left behind. Warrior shook the rib cage in the air and threw it down. He then took out his alien penis. He held it high and proceeded to piss on the fallen crumpled body of William Buck.

Alien urine (which is a great name for a band) landed all over him, which made this a horrible way to go. It went in his mouth and all over. At one point, William looked beyond his own death scene and into the woods. He locked eyes on another person, watching his misery. Allair Buck, his sister, looked on in fright and horror. Tears streamed down her face as Matt covered her mouth with his hand in an attempt to hold back her sobs. There's nothing she could do but watch as her brother died in a pissy bloody mangle. William reached out towards her saying, "Allair..." Warrior followed William's stare to

Allair. They locked eyes. He saw that her swimsuit was on. Cardinal sin.

Warrior Alien spoke, "Aaahhh-Lairrrrr."

Warrior set fire to William's body. Fire erupted from his hand, setting William ablaze. William's last screams were heard as Warrior's stare was fixed on the sister of this torn up burn victim. Warrior Alien stared, "AaahhLaaiir."

The four young bodies watched out the window at all the carnage going on. Flashes of flickering flames danced across their faces. Alan paced as he thought hard.

Geoff asked, "What is it looking at?"

"I think that's Allair over there with Matt," Emily said.

Alan realized what was at stake, "Is Allair nude yet?"

Summer and Geoff looked confused.

"Was she naked the last time you saw her?"

Summer said, "I don't remember..."

Alan said, "Hopefully she's smart enough to get naked."

Back at the resort, Teddy and Jambalaya sat down to play chess. As they set up the board, a lady came to serve snacks and drinks. She was an older lady with large breasts.

"Thank you, darlin'."

Jambalaya said, "Much appreciated." Once the board was set and they are about to begin, Jambalaya sat back a moment and thought of something. "Why do the white pieces always move first?"

Teddy pondered it a moment, "Because otherwise how would the black pieces know what to do?" Teddy made his move, and the game began.

"That's a good point, ya gotta keep your eye on Whitey, and make sure you know what he's doing. If we make a move first, they'll just steal it from us like they did with the Blues." He made his next move. "Elvis Presley, my ass."

"I hope those college kids are alright, except for Bruce and his thugs, hoping they're not okay. I hope they're getting fucked in the ass by that crazy lumberjack." He moved.

"Oh Lordy, he gives me the heepy jeebies."

"One way or another, I hope that abusive bastard and his buddies are in trouble."

"Yeah well, Ol' Whitey's in trouble now. Check!" Teddy sat back in astonishment. How did he not see that coming?

Matt and Allair ran through the woods. They jumped over logs and ran under bushes until they finally got to a clearing where they took a breath and tried to compose themselves for a moment.

"Back there," Allair said. "That was my brother."

"Oh my god, I'm sorry. There's a ranger station not far from here. If we get there, we can call for help." She nodded at Matt's suggestion. He took her hand, and they continued running. Eventually they came upon a marker that informed that they were leaving the nudist resort. Matt gave Allair a knowing glance; they were going in the right direction. Ultimately, they arrived upon a shabby cabin. They entered.

Allair and Matt slowly crept in and looked around. There was a spooky look to the place, and strangely there was a smashed television set. "Hello?" Allair hollered as the door slowly closed behind the lovers. The outline of someone or something closed in behind them. As doom approached, a light came on.

Nigel Jackson saw them coming. He was a rugged-looking hunter, a man's man. His best friend was a 12-year-old bottle of scotch. He had a look in his eye like he'd seen and done things that most people have just read about. He was clearly a dominant alpha-male that was not to be messed with. "Hold it right there. You got two minutes to tell me what the hell you're doing in my woods with your tally whacker dangling in the wind."

Matt stumbled over his words, "We ahhh, just came from the Bare Bear..."

"Bare Bear is east of here, what you just stumbled upon is a big old can of mouth raping. I'd crawl over fifty good pussies to get to one pretty boy's asshole. Give me one good reason why I shouldn't use your pretty girlfriend's hair to wipe your anal blood off my cock."

Allair exclaimed, "Oh my gawd, we'll just be going then..."

"You're not going anywhere 'til I say so. What you all are standing on is a trapdoor. All I gotta do is take my foot of this here switch and you'll be telling your story to about fifty hungry rats. Now why are you here?"

Matt looked at Allair, then at this psychopath and said, "We were looking for the ranger station, we didn't mean to trespass."

"Why are you here?"

"Our friends need help," Matt said.

"I didn't ask about your friends; right now, you need help, and I ain't yer friend! Why are you here!?"

Allair couldn't take it anymore, "Maybe, because this monster just killed my brother!"

Nigel took his foot off the switch, lost in thought, "Monster you say, the aliens..." Matt and Allair screamed expecting to plummet down below. They fell down on their knees expecting the worst... but it never came. The madman started laughing, "Sorry to put the scaring in you guys never can be too careful out here in these woods. Lots of freaks and weirdos and as you saw *goddamn* aliens. Anyway, let me help you up." They all uncomfortably reacquainted each other with proper introductions. They felt he's an okay guy... Or was he?

"So, you are the reclusive Ranger Jackson?" Matt asked.

"Yes, sir, but you can call me Nigel. Again, I apologize, ma'am, perhaps I've been out here to long, and forgotten my manner entirely. Under normal circumstances I wouldn't say the G.D. phrase in front of a lady."

Matt questioned him, "G.D.?"

Nigel Jackson whispered back to him, "Goddamn."

Matt was perturbed by how after all the trash talk that this is what he was bothered about.

Allair changed the subject. "Ranger Jackson... Er, um, Nigel, can we use your phone? My brother..."

Nigel cut her off, "I'm sorry. Signals are never too good in the mountains. Plus, something recently shorted out all my radio frequency equipment. Weirdest darn thing... Was gonna drive into town tomorrow to get it looked at." He then tossed army camouflage pants at Matt.

"I respect your life choices, but this ain't the naked resort friend. Plus, you might get cold." Matt put them on. "Funny you mentioned the aliens. I was just thinking about them earlier." Allair noticed that the walls were covered in newspaper articles and interviews from eyewitnesses that spoke of accidents and missing people. He also had drawn sketches of all four major aliens that they had seen thus far: Bubbles, Warrior, Sticks, Noodle-Arms. He had been obsessed with them for years. "I've been aware of them and what they do. Maybe it's time I get off my duff, and I finish what my daddy started years ago." According to some articles that were on the wall, his father was a ranger too. Articles suggested he was killed by them as well.

Matt saw that Nigel took an axe off the wall and held it proudly. "I think you are just who we needed to talk to tonight," Matt said.

"This was my father's axe. Let's go kick some alien ass."

Back in the cabin, the furniture had been moved to block the doors, and the windows were blocked as well. Alan was sleeping uncomfortably; he was visibly tossing and turning while uttering uncomfortable sounds. Emily lightly shook him and said, "Wake up, are you okay? Looks like you were having a pretty bloody awful nightmare."

Alan woke suddenly. Geoff and Summer looked at him worried as well. "I dreamt I was in a horror novel, but the writer didn't know how to kill me off."

"Wow. That's weird..." Summers said. "Say, how long do you think it's safe to stay here?"

Geoff suggested, "At least till morning, right?"

"There are aliens out there! We should all stay here until at least the last chapter of the book," Alan yelled.

"Humor at a time like this," Emily tsked. "The whole world is collapsing around us and you're being cheeky."

"No, I passed out, woke up from a nightmare into an even worse nightmare. I'm trying to keep myself from going insane. Look." He stands and points to a window. He saw of something as it passed by.

"They know we're in here, basically trapped. They are just waiting for us to fuck up somehow." Geoff held Summer tightly as Alan talked. They looked to him for guidance and leadership. What a horrible predicament these people were in that they were looking to Alan for leadership. Surely, they were all doomed.

"I need to go to the restroom." Summer said cautiously. Geoff held her hand.

"I'm coming with you." They moved off toward the bathroom.

Once the door was closed Geoff turned water on in the bathtub and started splashing the liquid on his hair and face. Summer sat on the toilet and began to tinkle. She heard something far away. It called to her, "Summmmmmmmmrrrrrrrrrrr."

She looked around and saw that Geoff was preoccupied with sticking his head under water. The call continued, "Suuuuummmmmeeerrr." A look of calm passed over her face. She felt an acceptance, and she stood and opened the window.

Geoff pulled his head up and noticed what was happening, "What the hell, Summer? You got to close the window."

Summer replied as if in a daze, "No, don't you get it. Think; remember at the rock, they didn't hurt us. Remember the bubbles? How it felt? It was so good." They look at each other. "That was the best I've ever felt."

"They could have killed us back there."

Geoff gave in, "You're right; they only killed the douche bags. We are safe."

"Maybe Alan is wrong. He's a *nerd* and a *virgin*."

Geoff cut her off, "It's practically the same thing."

"Summmmmeeerrrrrrrrr," the words came again. They both turned toward the open window.

Summer dreamily said, "They are waiting for us. Maybe they've always been waiting for us." Bubbles began to blow into the room and filled it from the bottom up.

Geoff nodded and took the towel he had been using and wrapped it around his woman. A chill blew into the bathroom. Bubbles came in wildly. Both were lost in the sea of possibilities.

As bubbles began to trickle out from beneath the bathroom door, Alan began to write something down and Emily looked out the window. "I can't wait for daylight. I feel like everything will be better in the morning. Is that odd?"

Alan spoke as he wrote, "I'm not one to judge what's odd, I've seen things tonight that I've only read about in scary comic books."

Emily turned to him. "What are you writing?"

"I hope I'm wrong, but I have a feeling I might not see the morning. if that's the case, then I'm going to put down everything I know on paper."

Emily was not quite sure how to respond. "That's morbid and negative. Don't think like that."

"I just hope it helps the next... Hey, ARE THOSE BUBBLES?"

He dashed over to the door and swung it open just quick enough to see Bubbles the alien standing in the middle of the room. He looked in the direction of the open door. BLINK-BLINK went her big eyes. She sat on the edge of the bathtub with her legs kicking; she dropped down and started walking towards the door. She got closer and closer until at the last moment Alan slammed the door shut on her pink furry face.

"Shit, they got Summer and Geoff, and one of the monsters is in the bathroom."

"Oh, bloody hell, I better write a note too, because *we* are gonna die."

Banging erupted all over the cabin as if a great Wendigo was blowing and throwing a tantrum. They heard vague screams all around. Suddenly everything went still; it was quiet for a moment.

Alan and Emily looked out the main window in stunned, unwelcomed silence.

Geoff's face was tossed against the glass and he was so madly happy; it was disturbing seeing him with that maniac wide smile. He laughed, "Hahhhhh ha ha haaaaaaaaaa." He cackled for a while, and then bit off his own tongue. Blood gushed from the wound filling his mouth and he still was in complete ecstasy. He mumbled something, spitting blood on the window, and then he fell away. It appeared to be in his mind the greatest day of his life.

Alan and Emily barely could compose themselves before there was another being slammed against the window. Both averted their eyes. Neither wanted to look in the direction, especially after last time. Suddenly there was a loud smash of broken glass. They looked up to see an alien Noodle-arms stuck in the broken window. It squirmed and screamed to free itself. Beyond the body of Noodle-arms stood Nigel Jackson, the misguided major league ass-kicker doing what he did best. He stood there holding his ground with an ax in one hand and a balled-up fist as the other. He was not to be messed with.

"You want some? Come get some." The creatures were curious and crept out of the shadows. They began circling around Nigel; His clothes were glowing in their eyes. The clothes were an abomination; they were an affront to nature. "Who's next!? Step on up..." One of the aliens stepped up and flashed pointy long fingers while sniffing in deeply. "Sticks, I've been waiting for this."

Sticks swiped at him with its mighty long arms. Nigel batted at it with his axe, defending against both arms, and finally kicked him down. After Nigel broke his long alien fingers, he saw red and went crazy chopping away at him. Alien blood sprayed all around as Nigel continued to chop away at the long alien. Noodle-arms grabbed Nigel's arm, the one holding the axe. It pulled him backwards toward its open mouth. Nigel used his axe to prop open its jaws. It let him go in order to dislodge the obstruction. Nigel got to his feet and continued to employ various combat maneuvers with Noodle-Arms and Sticks. Nigel's strategy resulted in both aliens getting killed. Sticks in particular suffered horribly because Nigel managed to chop one arm completely off. During the battle, the little creature, Bubbles, laughed and enjoyed the show. Nigel was on the losing end. Nigel walked towards Bubbles with a surge of adrenaline; he was ready to finish her off with a large piece of a tree that he picked up. Before he could get to her, Warrior stepped out blocking the way. Out of the aliens, he was clearly the alpha male. Live a silverback. The true battle alien was there for destruction, the likes of which Nigel had never known. Surely this would be an epic battle. Nigel choked up on the thick tree branch and quickly smashed Warrior directly in his big stupid alien face. Warrior was shocked and stumbled backward into the darkness; presumably he died from the impact. Bubbles watched this and let out one bubble of fear. Nigel then ran over to a scared little alien who had tried its best to look adorable. He punted it far off into the darkness of the night. It screamed as it flew through the air, and eventually there was a thud when it hit something hard. While still in a blind rage, Nigel spun around pulling his knife from its sheath and stabbed viciously. Both Nigel and his victim fell to the Earth together. Nigel held Alan; he ran up on Nigel innocently and got fatally stabbed for it.

In his dying gasps Alan said, "You need to take this off." Alan tugged at Nigel's outfit.

Nigel half chuckled, "Goddamn, you nudists never give up."

Alan wasn't laughing. "I wrote this..." He pulled out the letter that held the secret that *the Aliens can only see clothes*. He put the letter into Nigel's hand.

"It's okay mate, we don't need this. I kicked all their asses, like a man," Alan was almost gone now.

"You're a real Alpha-badass, Liz woulda loved... you," Alan coughed.

"Who's Liz?" Alan couldn't answer, he was gone.

There was silence on the remaining team. Allair held on to Matt, Nigel stood over Alan's dead body, and Emily watched it all. They looked to each other and thought about what was lost as the first rays of sunlight begin to appear over the horizon. Finally, this hellish night was over; they survived the worst of it.

Or have they?

OR HAVE THEY???

Nigel walked ahead of the three others on the trail out of the wilderness and back toward the swimming pools, tennis courts, and joyful fleshy bodices. He had the folded-up paper that Alan presented to him in his last moments. He held it a moment, with a thoughtful expression on his face. In his life, he had done a lot of killing. Matt walked behind him; the two girls trailed further behind. All of them were clothed; Emily wore Nigel's jacket.

The overall mood was relieved terror. Matt moved up to Nigel, who put away Alan's note that he was reading. They walked and talked.

"Damn shame about your friend back there."

"Yeah, thank you Nigel. I'm trying to keep it together until we get back home."

"It's not your fault, there was a lot of craziness going on, and you really saved us." Nigel nodded in agreement before hearing Matt Stanton continue. "I'll make sure the police understand that it was an accident." Nigel gave him a look. "They'll hear about it straight from me. You did a lot of good back there. But for now," He whispered, "we need to keep it together for the women." Nigel looked straight ahead.

They walked a moment in silence. Matt smiled; he was comforted that the evil was gone. He thought of Allair as she and Emily walked together. Allair was emotionally sad and physically tore up from the night. Emily was determined to get her friend feeling better.

Emily jabbed Allair in the arm, "Did that little one fart a bubble?"

Allair smirked a maddening smile, "I think it did." They both laughed almost manically. It felt good to release all the stress of the night. Matt turned to look back at them and was pleased to see Allair happy even for a moment.

"Allair," Emily laughed, "Oh brother."

"Brother..." Allair looked off, remembering William, and she suddenly got choked up.

"I'm really sorry about your brother." Emily comforted her friend. "I know we didn't always see eye to eye, but he was a really good man. If there is a heaven, you can be sure he's there in paradise." Allair started tearing up. She had lost someone who really knew her. Emily called out to the men. "Hey, men, we need a women's bathroom break, and it's gonna be awhile." The men stopped walking.

"We'll be right here" Then Nigel advised "Don't go too far. We understand, so please take your time." The ladies walked off; Emily held a crying Allair.

When the men were all alone, Nigel continued, "So Matt, you're planning ongoing to the cops, eh? Can't say I like that idea." Matt noticed the mood change between them. "I was planning on letting you live long enough for you to watch me fuck those two little sluts in every opening they got and maybe make some new ones." Matt was alarmed and started to back away. Nigel rushed him and stabbed him deep in his chest. He held him close and spoke to his ear. "Looking forward to slicing your bitch from her cunt to her throat," Nigel threw Matt down. He laid there on the dirt, gasping and bleeding. "Killing you will be almost as satisfying as killing that nerd was back there." Matt looked at him in astonishment; the psychopath stepped on his throat, "But I'm going to take my time with you." Nigel pulled the paper from his pocket and dropped it on his chest. "Your boyfriend wanted you to dirt, see this. "Maybe you can read it while I'm digging out your dirt hole with my dick; ain't nobody gonna save you now, don't you get it?" Nigel quickly stabbed Matt again; twice this time just to show he can. "Think I was killing those aliens to help you? That was fun, just like cutting you now is fun, just like what I'm gonna do to those two little girls is fun." Nigel plunged the knife blade deep, and then twisted the innards, again.

Nigel stood and walked away from Matt; he enjoyed watching him squirm. Nigel looked at the blood on the knife and licked it. "I always liked the taste of pussy blood." Nigel wiped the rest of the blood from Matt's chest wounds on his hand and turned his back. He was in some sort of ecstasy and closed his eyes as he puts his hand down his pants and caressed his manhood. His sexual animalistic urge was uncontrollable.

Over his shoulder, Matt read Alan's last note. Suddenly he understood. As best as he could, he started taking off the only clothing he had left on... the camo pants this murderer gave him earlier. After a short struggle, he is naked and safe from one of the vicious killers; Matt laid there and tried not to die from wounds inflicted by the other one.

Nigel noticed Matt's struggle, "Getting ready for me, you little faggot? Hope you got the squirts, because diarrhea is the only lube you're gonna get." Before he could get his homoerotic hands on the nudist, a huge towering mass made its presence known. Warrior Alien broke in from the brush and with its vision saw that Matt had no evilness on him, but Nigel was glowing like mad; he lunged at him. Warrior took him off in the wilderness for his punishment. Warrior was still bleeding slime from his earlier encounter with Nigel, but it wasn't fatal. Just as the two disappear into the woods, the women came running to Matt's side.

"Oh my god, what happened to you?" Allair hollered. "We heard screaming. Where's Nigel?" Matt was trying to hold on.

Emily went into lifesaving mode; it fit her training since she was going to nursing school. She got the blood to slow down. "We have to get you out of here, it's not far now to the resort, right?"

Matt ignored her and plead, "Thing still alive, have to get naked. Both of you..." He passed the note to them.

Allair was confused, "What does it say? The Alien did this to you? Where's Nigel? What the hell happened?" Matt pulled her close.

He had blood coming from his mouth as he forced the words, "He did... this..." Allair was shocked, just when she thought things were better. Emily held up the note and read aloud: "It's from Alan... I watched him write it earlier."

DEAR FRIENDS,

IF YOU WANT TO STAY ALIVE, UNLIKE MYSELF, WHO IS MOST

LIKELY DEAD BY NOW, YOU NEED TO KEEP YOUR CLOTHES OFF. TEDDY WAS RIGHT. THEY SEE YOU BY FABRIC.

HOPE THIS KEEPS YOU ALIVE LONGER.

SINCERELY, ALAN.

PS - I DIED A VIRGIN. FUCK.'"

Emily dropped the note and tossed Nigel's jacket off like a bad habit, making herself fully natural again. Lovely dark skin fully on display left the only clothed person left in danger. Allair. She looked at them and recognized this with one more creature out there, there wasn't much choice. Allair turned away from Matt and Emily and disrobed publicly for the first time with her back to them. When she was fully nude, she was a little embarrassed. Matt looked at her and mumbled, "Beautiful."

Emily helped Matt hang on her shoulder, and they took the first few steps on the path out of this hell. As they begin to leave, Allair looked back at her restrictive swimsuit that she wore for most of the night.

She also looked at the trail of green alien blood that led away from the attack. *It can bleed.* Finally, she picked up Nigel's disregarded knife and remembered her brother.

"No, I'm not leaving. I have to finish this." Matt and Emily stopped and looked at her. "You said it was injured, right? I'm going to finish it off."

Emily argued, "Allair, that thing saved Matt's life from the psycho Ranger. We are all naked now. Balls, beaver, whatever, you have nothing to worry about. It can't see you. We know how to stay alive now. So, let's just get out of here."

"No! That thing is still out there. He killed all those people, including my brother. He pissed on him while I watched, and I did nothing because I was scared. You know what, Emily? You know what? I'm not scared anymore. He can't see me. That thing is not going to hurt anyone else." She kissed Matt. "Matt, I know how you feel about me.

I want you to know I feel the same way too. I love every moment I get to spend with you. I love you so much." After a brief romantic moment, she snapped back to militant attention and looked directly at Emily. "Get out of here! Do not stop, please. When you get to the resort, call the cops. Tell them I'm in here kicking some alien ass."

Emily stopped her, "There's something I need to tell you first. It's about William and me..."

Allair looked at Matt, dying. "Not now, please get him out of here."

Emily reluctantly nodded, and they walked down the trail. Allair had her back to them, and she was already thinking of tracking this son-of-a-bitch. She saw some mud nearby and ceremonially wiped it on her naked body. She stood fully nude, a confidant warrior in her own right, and she looked ready both physically and mentally to kick some ass. *That alien was going to pay.*

Allair proclaimed aloud, "Mommy's going hunting."

Allair tracked the green spots of alien blood. The trail led her through various obstacles. She moved over logs, passed trees, and she waded through a stream. She finally came to a clearing where the alien stood. It had its back to her. There was a puddle of green blood near it. It appeared to be dying. This was not far from the entrance to its portal. It was trying to make its way home. Allair knew it was wounded badly, and she can see all the blood it lost. She felt sure of herself, especially since it couldn't see her. She held her knife out in front of her and called to it, "Hey, demon. I see you. I SEE YOU."

Warrior switched from an appearance of looking wounded and injured to a sudden smirk of satisfaction raked on its leathered worn out ancient head. It rose and stood tall with its back to her and turned around slowly, revealing that it was not injured much at all. It had been a ruse, and it was holding a severed arm from Sticks that dripped with green blood. This alien warrior had tricked her.

They locked eyes. Warrior tossed aside the arm and let out an animalistic combat yell. It taunted her by waving its huge spikes arms; it knew if she had come this far it was for a war. However, Allair was no dummy. This monster was almost completely healthy, and as much as she wanted vengeance, she was just a naked girl covered in mud in the woods with a knife. She had no combat training.

"Allair..." She whispered to herself. "This is a bad idea." Warrior leaned in and got closer to the knife, daring her to make the first move. "You can still catch up with Matt and Emily if you..."

Warrior was close to the knife and lets out a thunderous roar. She decided to get outta there. Allair turned and ran, dropping her knife in her adrenaline haze to escape. She ran as fast as she could. She looked over her shoulder for Warrior and tripped and fell. Allair hit her head and everything faded around her.

Through the haze she heard a faint voice in the darkness whispering, "Alllairrr..." The voice of the giant monstrous being, Warrior was talking to her.

No, not him, another… The voice is clearer now.

"Allairrr..."

Her eyes opened. Allair saw her brother William Buck standing in front of her. He was soaking wet. His hair, his shirt all covered in liquid, but it was him and he appeared to be alive. Allair gave him a big hug. "Oh, it's really you."

"My dear sister..."

Allair wondered, "Does this mean I'm dead too?"

"Not yet. You still have a chance." Allair struggled to comprehend this all. Where was she? What was this? "Look, we don't have a lot of time. I want you to know I believe in you, I always have. You are my sister, and I love you. Life is one moment; you can decide if you'll spend that moment running or spend that moment fighting. If you choose to run, then you spend eternity running." She was lost in his words as he spoke. His words resonated within her. "That demon Warrior out there represents fear. If you run from it now, you'll always look over your shoulder for it, be it in the closet, or under your bed. You are too strong to run. Kill it off. Kill off the fear and live your life for yourself! Do you understand?"

"Yes." She nodded then asked, "Before I go back, what's heaven like?" William got uncomfortable.

"Heaven? Well, I don't know much about heaven since I'm stuck haunting the woods here with a bunch of naked ghosts." Just then the spirits of Alan and Liz walked by, each proudly displaying a sign of how they died, Alan was gutted with fleshy tubes hanging from his openings and Liz had deep scars and scratches all over her body. Both were still naked as the day they were born; they happily held each other's hands. They were together in the afterlife. They noticed William standing, but didn't see Allair from her spot on the ground, "Hi William, beautiful day!"

William turned to acknowledge them begrudgingly. "Hi, Alan. Hi Liz." He turned back to Allair, pointing secretly in their direction. He motioned with his hands, like, *really? See what I mean.* Once they walked away, he continued with a sigh, lamenting his lost years. "Listen Allair, just because you're breathing doesn't mean you're alive." He paused to get this point to her. "Are you alive, or are you just breathing?"

"I'm alive."

"Then prove it. Live your life with no regrets."

She nodded.

"One more thing..." He leaned over to her and whispered something very deliberate to her ear as he faded away. She answered by putting her hand over his heart on his wet squishy shirt in an affirmative action. After she removed her hand, she smelled it.

"Is that...?" He was almost completely gone from her plane of existence.

"Yes. It's urine. Alien pee-pee." William disappeared completely from her dream state to the normal world. The last image of her brother was his freaking out as he spun a semi-circle with his arms raised high, "HONESTLY REALLY!? I'm covered in piss; tell me, DID HE LIVE OFF ASPARAGUS? Why won't it ever dry?" William was not happy. He was NOT *Resting in Peace-* he was *Resting in Piss.* Yes, you just read that.

Allair opened her eyes and knew she was still in mortal danger. She did not know how long she'd been out. She smelled her hand. She became comfortable that she is in reality now with renewed purpose, because it didn't smell like pee. She sat up.

She walked with a purpose.

She picked up her lost knife.

Fight or Flight? I choose fight.

Her face was very serious; she was on her way with purpose. She appropriately still had mud on her face; She was hunting.

The Alien Warrior was picking up scraps of clothing and putting them in his human flesh skin bag that Sticks had earlier. He almost looked bored. This time he was a victim. A primal scream erupted, and in a moment Allair was on his back. She stabbed his chest with the knife. Spurts of green blood shot out in stabbing motions between his hard scales. After taking some serious damage, he threw her off his back hard. She moved back to blend in with the trees, knowing he couldn't fully see her.

He yelled and was ready to finish this. He pulled out some clothing and tossed it in her direction to hopefully capture her bodice in cloth. She grabbed a blanket that he threw from the air and tossed it over a pile of tree limbs. As she hoped, he rushed in like a dumb rhino and got nothing but splintered wood for his trouble.

This repeated a few times, during which Allair found a bottle of insect repellent nearby and she held on to it. After the second or third time, she had him smash into clothes. He stopped short of the covering and knew she was nearby. Warrior faked the run and instead hit her, tossing her back. He noticed clothes on his arm and picked at it.

When he looked up, she was gone. He looked all over, inspecting various clothing pieces for signs of his victim. Finally, he gave up. He believed that she had perhaps retreated.

He went to pick up the skin bag again, but it was heavier than before. Allair Buck popped out of it and sprayed him in his face. He choked and fell to his knees. He eventually fell back, choking. She was pleased that her plan had worked better than she imagined. She tossed the can aside and grabbed the biggest rock she could find. Allair raised it high and smashed Warrior in his face over and over and over again.

She breathed heavily and sweat dripped from her brow while she pulled the boulder down on the alien with maximum impact. Warrior squirmed like a squashed bug. Eventually he stopped moving. All was quiet, but it was interrupted by a sound of trickling water. Allair leaned forward and whispered into what she thought was Warrior's ear, "This is for my brother."

A line of urine ran down his chest from where she was squatting. She marked her victory like an animal. She stood up. Warrior looked at her with its smashed face and mumbled, "Allairrrr."

She looked at the bug spray bottle and then saw a book of matches that must have fallen out of some clothing.

Allair walked out of the wilderness trails beyond the Bare Bear Family Nudist Resort. Behind her, the alien warrior screamed as fire consumed his exoskeleton and meat between it. He burned, and she did not care. She had no sympathy. She was a different woman now. She could see the front of the facility and noticed a police car. There were cops outside talking with Emily and Teddy. There was also an ambulance, which Allair imagined had medical personnel inside tending to Matt's injuries.

Everyone took notice of the traumatized woman; she was bloody, beaten and muddy in patches all over her nude body. The cops stopped what they are doing and one ran up to her, attempting to put a cloth covering around her nudity. Allair let it fall behind her; she would have none of it.

The cop picked up the cloth, "I know what sort of place this is, I just thought you might want..."

"You thought wrong," Allair responded.

"Ma'am what happened? Is there anyone else out there following you?"

"There's nothing out there anymore. It's over now."

"Well, don't you dare go far. I'll have more questions for you."

Cops talked again with Emily and Teddy. Various residents, onlookers, and Jambalaya looked on. Allair was not feeling shy or embarrassed; she was comfortable in her own skin, and she was a changed woman proud to be au naturel.

She made her way toward the ambulance. She saw Matt being treated by medical personal. They wore medical scrubs and were working on him; he was in better condition and looked to be alert. She noticed the contrast to their first meeting. He was no longer the nude model; she was exposed as he lay covered by the blanket. He looked at her through the window. She was nude; he was not. He smiled, she smiled.

The sun burned brightly as a naked gathering of college-aged friends played volleyball on the San Diego beach. The waves flowed lightly beyond them, playing as fully nude surfers caught the bigger waves further out. Families of all ages frolicked and played at this modern-day Garden of Eden. The ball bounced off to the side, rolling off the sand and into brush. A naked blonde noticed right away and started running after it, her body toned and tanned, tight and athletic.

Chrissi yelled, "I got it!"

She picked up a sun hat from her blanket and hustled off, looking through the brush away from her friends. She found the ball, but before she could pick it up, bubbles rose up. She looked up through the bubbles and saw something. She screamed. Nigel Jackson looked back at her through the bubbles, pulling up his newly acquired alien pincher claw. He was remade in their image and now is more evil than ever.

11

AT THE FEET OF THE MASTER

MY INTERVIEW WITH CLIVE BARKER

Originally published in the Bram Stoker winning collection *It's Alive: Bringing Your Nightmares to Life,* Edited by Joe Mynhardt and published by Crystal Lake Publishing.

When I was a child I gravitated towards the larger hardcover bound books at my community library. The very highest level of the deviant and forbidden was always his words, always his. I'd look thru *The Books of Blood* and quiver in my little boy boots at what sort of man would create this. Who is he? These images came to life in my youthful impressionable mind, what sort of man indeed. My interest in checking out all of his adult fiction brought the ire of the librarian who told me emphatically I was forbidden to read the works of Clive Barker unless I had a parent say it was okay. With my mother standing across the checkout table a day or two later, that self-imposed dictator of censorship was confronted and as she backed down from her earlier judgment she told my mother something I never forgot, "Well fine – he can read Clive

Barker, but know this, he'll either grow up to be a great horror writer, or a serial killer."

I never killed anyone, but I did begin writing and occasionally I thought of him. I met him in person for the first time at Dark Delicacies, the classic brick and mortar shop dedicated to all things macabre, located in Burbank, California. I remember clearly so desperately wanting to separate myself from the regular fans standing in line, to let him know I wasn't just an admirer but rather a peer. A fellow dark dreamer, however I was still a peer holding books for him to sign just like everyone else, I had to find a way... I decided on a few choice statements to show how I was different. When I had my moment with him we connected over my unusual musings, and he invited me to his side of table, (it had worked!) I sat next to my guru as he finished signing and doodling art for the rest of the fans. He invited me to pose for a collection of photography, but I chickened out because it was very erotic. We exchanged emails for years after that, advice, and notes about the industry as my career blossomed. He even gave me a blurb on my writing which graced the cover of my first book. Getting to know him as I have, I can say without a doubt he is a very giving, charming and unique individual. Nobody sees the world like this visionary. While at the same time, he is human and after being bedridden from toxic shock for nearly three years he was the first to tell me that he isn't the man he used to be. No matter, Clive Barker is an artist we all can relate too and still has the fire in his eyes. Having an excuse to meet back up with him for this book was a joy.

Segments of this interview were recorded over the course of three visits around Halloween 2018 at his home in Beverly Hills, California. I hope you enjoy it.

TIM CHIZMAR: Welcome!

CLIVE BARKER: Isn't it, I who should welcome you?

We both laugh.

TC: Very nice to be here with you again.

CB: Very nice indeed.

TC: What is it that you love about the writing process?

CB: Well, I don't always love it, it can be a pain in the frickin ass, you know this- there are days where the page seems to recede from you, you know I handwrite everything obviously (*Clive motions to stacks of papers*) and there are days where the pen can't make contact to the paper. Or if it does it's not a good word that appears and that happens, now on the other hand there are days when a lucidity that is unearned by any method that I know anyway is in your pen: actually head heart pen, right? I think that's the three-part journey. Yeah? For me as a handwritten. Actually, from heart to head to hand It goes to heart first because if I don't feel it, I have no interest in telling it, does that make sense?

TC: Yes of course, are you more plot-driven or character-based in your writing?

CB: I don't think there's a difference. If there's no character there's no plot.. if there's no plot the characters just stand there.

TC: Please tell me, do your characters ever surprise you?

CB: All the fucking time, absolutely but that's not the same as difference between plot and characters is it With respect, plot is a way to move a narrative toward a conclusion which you have either morally, or philosophically or spiritually predetermined: I want to give stories to people. A river that moves really fast carries larger stones, the stone represents the weight of philosophical spiritual content, the narrative should move forward, yeah? And there should be an inevitability about it, you don't know where its going but you know its going somewhere. You're in the hands of somebody who has begun to tell a tale that he or she is driven to tell. What drives me are three things: Curiosity, Curiosity, Curiosity. I am spiritually curious – I am sexually curious – geographically curious.. That is to say that very few of my narratives if any, now that I think of it happen in the same place …. I never thought about that before… I've written, I dunno 40 books.. I don't think I've ever written a story set in the same city. I love new places. I've written about Liverpool my hometown I think actually twice, once in a short story and once in *Weaveworld* so I have been back there twice but by and large I like to go to new places. People are different from each other and very often places are different from each other. I'm astonished that white people write only about white people, largely speaking, broadly speaking, straight people right largely about only straight people, gay men tend to write about other gay men, gay women tend to write about other gay women.. if I were a wrestler id want to write a book about boxing! If I was a boxer I'd want to write about masturbation, I don't know whatever it was going to be. I don't think there's a reason – for me it's journeying. Of one kind or another and you want to journey places you haven't been before. I'm not good in crowds to be perfectly honest. I have to be in some faintly altered state of soul to feel comfortable about wandering around. I can get into an altered state just by getting naked.

TC: I certainly understand that. Tell me Clive, what advice would you give to young writers? Somebody new, just starting out?

CB: A filmmaker came to Kubrick and said, "I want to make films. Mr. Kubrick what should I do?" Buy a camera, he had said.

TC: I believe James Cameron said that to a fan as well, so in other words are you saying people just over think it?

CB: Yeah, what is there to think about? If you're going to write, then fucking write.

TC: I love it!

CB: People come up to me at conventions, and say things like I have a great idea for a novel, I say good when did you start writing it? Oh you're gonna write it I'll just take 50%. They say that so often, so often, and I say- you really don't get this do you? Its not about having an idea – T.S. Elliot, said its not good enough to be drunk on a Friday night writing a poem you have to be sober at 9AM on a Monday morning writing a poem, writing from an altered state is earned by writing. You don't get drunk and then write, firstly it won't be any good, and secondly you'll be an alcoholic by the end of the week. You've got to work from a place of joy in the process of writing. And the problem with that is that very often the process isn't joyful. Because its hard fucking work..

TC: Yes, it sure is.

CB: ..and because you mess up, right? You've been to all these places yourself so we are talking writer to writer here – I think you may end up answering this question yourself because between the two of us we probably know about all the pitfalls and all the highs. The highs when they come along are mind-blowing, aren't they?

TC: Yes, I was just the guest speaker for a screenwriter event in Hollywood and it felt like joy.

CB: Although let's be honest, a screenplay is an invitation to a dance it's not the dance.

TC: Yes, that's correct, I always say there are three movies, the one you write, the one you shoot and the one they edit. Three completely different movies.

CB: There's four, the one they review! There's a 5th, the one they review 30yrs after…

TC: This is fascinating.

CB: I can testify to that because *Cabal* and Nightbreed and the Directors Cut came out last year with the 25min they had cut put back in again and the movie that people despised, they now adored. Yes, and there's a 6th one! The one they review when you're dead. In other words what I'm saying is a movie seems fixed doesn't it? But its protean because people change and peoples response as well. People's response to narrative changes. What we thought *Hansel and Gretel* was about when we first heard it is not what *Hansel and Gretel* is about. Right, Its about two children lost in a forest almost eaten alive and who were put their by their mother and father Bruno Bettelheim writes about this, about fairy tales subtectual life of a fairytale now if that's true of a fairy tale in ten pages long, how much more true is it in a long elaborate short story or a novel. The complexity of possibilities that can and do happen. You know it was Socrates, or some Greek, that said you never step into the same river twice. Yeah, that's true, true for two reasons number one the water has moved on and number two you are not the same person who last stepped into that river. So, when you start the next sentence of your book you're not going to be the person you were when you left it. You had a conversation, you got into a depressed state, you got into a joyful state, and you feel angry, you do feel, whatever it is… I am given things often in the night, an example: *Brother Plato right or wrong said the tribe where I belong, is a family of souls in two, me a half another you, lets stay* *together one tonight, and prove our brother Plato right.* Now I woke up in the middle of the night, wrote that down and fell asleep again. I knew I'd written it in the morning, but I didn't have any clue as to where it came from. It's a very elaborate rhyme scheme, *Brother Plato right or wrong said the tribe where I belong, is a family of souls in two, me a half another you, lets stay together one tonight, and prove our brother Plato right.* So the first line echoes the last line *Brother Plato right or wrong* and *prove our brother Plato right.* So the structure, you can't get into it, it's a lot you can't polish it, there's nothing to polish and somebody gave me that. I'm not someone that believes my subconscious is a genius (*he laughs*) I don't, I don't.. something is in the air around us I'm speaking now of everybody, but more so those who are willing to enhance their creativity with doing it a lot there's something around us that is – how do I say this – Its like somebody doesn't allow access to these things is like a sealed steel ball, somewhere locked in the middle of that steel ball is their soul – you, me.. we may still be steel balls but our steel balls are full of holes! Right, the energies which are around us all the time are being drawn in through those holes to what's in the middle which is us. All I am doing all the time is making sure the holes are clean and open and wide and that's the most I can do as an artist. I can't practice it. It's not like a violin I can just do it, and if I do it often enough well enough meticulously enough the powers that surround us the divine things that the energies which allow for creation.

TC: What of overt sexuality, which seems to be a reoccurring theme for you in your work…

CB: Sexuality is a very fucking complicated thing.

We both laugh.

TC: How do you handle depression or life's bullshit in your work?

CB: We all have bad times. Hollywood is based on lies to a large extent. What could be is not necessarily what will be. But we can undo the curse. By large I believe people don't believe there are ways to undo the curse anymore. I think Trump has something to do with that, our situation globally has something to do with that, that we are watching the world fall apart and nobody seems to give a fuck.

TC: You have worked in so many mediums, comics, books, movies, video games is there any interconnectivity? For example, now everything comes from graphic novels…

CB: Pity isn't it? My point is I can't paint at the top of my talent in a comic, I can't write a poem in a comic, I can't talk about… look I love comics but they are a very limited medium, very limited aren't they? I fear that the explosion of movies based on comics will kill comics because people won't want to read static images in which someone who isn't Robert Downey Jr is playing Iron Man. When was the last time you read *Prince Valiant* the comic book or *Flash Gordon?*

TC: Never. I saw Flesh Gordon…

CB: So did I. *(laughs)* Serious question though, my point is these were extraordinary comic books.

TC: Okay.

CB: And you don't know what they are anymore. Yet there is a new Flash Gordon on Netflix, in other words… comics are seen as source material for experiments.

TC: Perhaps they are seen and used as a storyboard.

CB: You are right, they are a storyboard. For me things always come back to books, always. Look at Jack Kirby, I knew Jack very little, but he did six pages a day, when you look at it now it's awesome but it does look exactly like what you just said. It looks like storyboards. Yet it isn't, it's the outpourings one of the most extraordinary imaginations of the 20th century and if you were to ask somebody who created Iron Man most people would say Robert Downey Jr.

TC: Wow.

CB: Don't you think? Do you think anybody would say – Oh ah Jack Kirby – Do you think anybody would actually say that now?

TC: No the average ticket-going fan… I agree.

CB: If we are going by numbers, I think the average ticket-going fan couldn't give a flying fuck what the origins of the material are.

TC: That's a shame

CB: But don't you think it's true?

TC: I'm a Comic-Con guy, so my circle…

CB: Yeah I know you, this isn't about you, and we value *Dr.Strange* you know who made *Dr.Strange* Steve Ditko's work redefines what magic is in comic books. His work is groundbreaking, the designs of the environments and not just the characters. How many people know who made *Dr. Strange* ?

TC: Well, that's a shame.

CB: But do you agree?

TC: Sadly. Let me ask you another question. You've created video games such as Jericho and others, what is that process like?

CB: I had the best time because I got to do the designs; I got to do the story. Then the stuff I don't really like, the technical stuff, I didn't have any hand in. I'd have gladly done more but it's a very strange business. I never understood the politics of it. It's like working for a studio in which you never meet the people that head up the studio. I did three in total.

TC: Do you have an ending in mind? Do all the paths lead to the same big bad guy?

CB: There is no ending is there? Lots of endings, you play it out, in theory it's like a Chess game, no two are exactly alike.

TC: So you just create the pieces and let them go at it?

CB: It's like making a map for which there are diverse routes. Then you create the characters and say have at it guys. So much of it is trickery, saying BOO! and I'm not a big fan of that. I've been surprised at how intense some of the games get though, incredibly violent.

TC: Was it ever your intention for Pinhead to become a sex symbol?

CB: Nooo not really...

TC: I know I should call him the Hell Priest that was never your intention for him to be given that name.

CB: Its fine, everyone knows him that way anyway. I don't find monsters very sexy, I'm thinking of there are any exceptions to that.

TC: Certainly Hellraiser is very sexual, right?

CB: But sexual is not the same as sexy is it? He's very sexualized but he talks about pain and pleasure in a detached way. You don't get the impression he's getting off every Wednesday. He's very cold and yet you get told what is true by the people who read you, am I right? Its people's response to the work that tells you what he work is. It never occurred to me that these rather ominous figures would ever be attractive for example his is not a face you could touch. By his very nature its gonna hurt. Not in a good way. Plus his personality is not fun. For me, to be sexy is to be fun. He is not fun. He is judgmental, he is cold and I think that nature is opposite to sexy. Not opposite sexual..

TC: If I can be honest, I was terrified when I saw him.

CB: When you first saw him? I love that. That's exactly what was intended.

TC: I wasn't "tee hee" scared like with a Freddy Krueger I was legitamitely terrified because if you're in a room and the box opens and the doorways open what are you gonna do? You're fucked.

CB: That's interesting. So it was the box that was the first indicator yes? Have you seen the new Sabrina? I'm in it, well second season, but my paintings are in it a lot. They used a lot of my paintings. I haven't seen it yet but they used a version of my box called a different kind of configuration puzzle box on the show. For Hellraiser I had a story about raising powers but how could I show that without using images we've seen a thousand times, I didn't want to show drawing in chalk while speaking backwards in latin or whatever so eventually I remembered that my grandfather brought back from China where he was a ships cook a puzzle box a very simple one and nothing as elaborate as in the movie but it was wooden and it was about the same size as the box. It fascinated me cause there was only one way to make it work, I've long since lost it. It was my grandmothers and she'd passed and so on but I thought wow wouldn't that be cool because raising something is the opening of a door and solving a puzzle is in a way an opening of a door. So using this as a symbolic door-opener, like a key almost made sense and then I found this guy Simon Sayce whos passed away of cancer, but when he was about your age, we sat down and thought how do we make this like nothing that's been seen before? He obsessed on it for months. He gave me something that is as central a part of the mythology as Pinhead is.

TC: The circular story-telling, the way it opens and closes with the passing of the box, I've watched it lots of times and listened to your commentary with Ashley Lawrence. I loved it but it terrified me and that's why I went back and revisited it as an adult to see why it scared me so much.

CB: What was the answer?

TC: Loss of power, and the amazing sequence with the engineer chasing her down the hallway, that was just about the most terrifying thing I've ever seen because its so close and the unpredictability of the box and the doorways, I thought for sure it could close before she got to the end!

CB: Yeah, absolutely, its even set up like it could happen, I felt that – we made that for nine-hundred thousand bucks, which sounded like a shit ton of money when they said it at first, but it wasn't a lot and I've always felt when you don't have very much you try harder. It was stuck together with spit and tape.

TC: It's a masterpiece it really is great.

CB: Well, thank you, I want to offer these three things as putting myself out of the picture for a moment. I was blessed with special effects such that nobody would expect for that scale of picture. Particularly in the designs, in the way I think, Pinhead once seen is never forgotten, I think.

TC: Chatterer too..

CB: They are nightmares. I had a great DP who I could persuade to turn lights off. That time movies were over lit you remember? Look at Poltergeist now it's like a Disneyland movie. Bright, bright, bright, even something like Fright Night, which is a movie I love, nevertheless, bright! I said to him, I know you're not going to like this but we are going to turn lights off. There's a shot for instance – I remember this because we had a big argument over it – close-up of the guy who was playing Frank hunched in the corner of the upstairs room when he's not really fully brought back and he turns and looks at Julia through the door there and he says "I need more blood" or something, and there was a lot of light on him and I said we'll do it your way but then lets shoot it by turning off everything but one light. It was a rim light shot basically. In dailies the next day he said – "Okay

I'm convinced." We turned off a lot of lights, it had two advantages, it made the thing look bigger, because with a lot of darkness you're not sure what's there. Secondly, it made it look kinda classy. The most important thing I had was Chris Young, I had music.

TC: The music was powerful.

CB: Powerful and bigger, much bigger than a movie of that scale would normally be.

TC: Creepily cheerful, that sound like a toy box.

CB: Absolutely, the little Chinese box from my grandfather had a little "ding, ding, tinkle, tinkle" noise inside it, I mentioned that to Chris and he put that in it. He had a sense of grandeur, when the opening credits go, we were used to Carpenter's two fingers the Halloween deal, no argument about that, it works but it wasn't big and I had seen The Fury with a John Williams score and it had this magnificence to it and I think it's a much better film than people give it credit for. I'm not a big DePalma fan across the board but I think it's a great picture. I thought, Wow if I could get that kind of sound. We had this tiny room with a piano and we went through this for weeks, he instantly got it and wanted to make it as big as possible. We called in favors from everywhere to have a much bigger orchestra than we could afford. As a consequence, the picture grows; it just grows in scale because the music does that for you.

TC: It all just stays with the viewer with so many layers.

CB: It's about something. It's about a family. I've always said the scariest line in the movie is "Come to Daddy" because firstly it's not her father, secondly it implies something incestuous is about to happen. It's certainly sexual what he's saying to her and for one terrible moment you think maybe she'll succumb to this, then she gets to scrape his face and you see there's another body below there. First thing I said on the day of reading the thing, I said to everyone this is not funny.

TC: Why do you think so many people fight horror from being mainstream?

CB: Mainstream horror is only acceptable to reviewers if it doesn't take itself seriously. In other words if it seems to be mocking itself or if it seems to be done for the buck, reviewers say, "That proves me right. This is a worthless genre." The whole idea of coming to peace with horror means that you are taking the idea of horror in the world as something that is real I don't think most people want to think about that. That's okay, because I don't want to say I'm like you, because I'm not like you.

TC: It's a shame people still think horror writers are psychos or crazy.

CB: But let me offer this, if we were normal…

TC: You know what Oscar Wilde said? "The only normal people you know are the people you don't know that well?"

CB: Right, right, right, which is the equivalent of Groucho's "I don't want to be a member of a club that would have me as a member."

Shared laugh.

TC: I love Groucho.

CB: So do I.

EXTRAS

For anyone interested, here are some extra rewards on each story's back information. Where it was published before this book, if it was, who I was thinking of when I wrote it... etc.

"UNLOCKING THE DOOR" is a short fable I solely wrote for an anthology of gothic vampire stories. I'd queried the publisher after being impressed with some of his prior works, and he liked my idea and gave me the approval. Alas, after I'd completed it, I was informed the publisher paid far below industry rates, and thus it was not worth it to me to agree to give it away practically for free. It was partially my fault for not discussing payment upfront and it's a lesson I shall never fall victim to again. Writing isn't a hobby, it's my job. I have some friends in the corner of the world, so I reached out to them in my research and I loved falling into the gypsy world.

"D'MON" is a cult classic of mine. I completely "fan boy" out at the thought of a Jamaican battle-scarred demon fighting against the pressures of his birthright commitment to collect souls in Hell. Sadly, some beta readers have mentioned a similarity to *Hellboy*, which wasn't my intention. I love the imagery and feel a bit of a *Star Wars* meets *NightBreed* style feeling which I hope comes across... I elaborated on this theme while changing it up a tad in a full-length novel called *Soul Traitor*. Buy it now.

"CHUPACABRE" was written as part of a longer story I lost interest in. It's pretty weird, but I hope I captured the ideas from my days in Mexico and Los Angeles well enough. Marky is a composite of many of those poor souls that will do anything to be famous. They don't necessarily want to act, sing, write or put any effort into a craft; they just want to be famous for being themselves. It's a self-defeating dead-end road, let me tell you...

"CARGO" came out originally in the collection *18 Wheels of Horror* by *Big Time Books*, hence the mention of the editor Eric Miller in the story. It's pretty funny, but when I was presented with the premise after a meeting of the Los Angeles chapter of the *HWA*, I said, "I can do that!" I especially love the part about the Ninja Turtles, and a nod to Dwight Yoakum, whom I dig. I channeled parts of Stone Cold Steve Austin and a hardass biker I knew in LA.

"FARKELBERRY FORREST CEMETERY" was ridiculous. I just ran with a silly, goofy, unnatural concept of *what if a guy rose from the dead but couldn't get out of his coffin and he's not alone*. The voice of the worm was inspired by a silly voice my friend Diane and I used to do when playing around. It was originally published in a collection called *Halloween Tales* put out by *Omnium Gatherum*. During its initial release, I did a signing at a horror convention called Scare LA, and sold out of all the copies in one day. I love talking with fright fans, and for me it was more about the connections than selling.

"DEAD AND BREAKFAST" was adapted from a Hitchcock'ian influenced short film script I'd written. I envisioned it being shot in black and white, but unfortunately (like so many best laid plans) it never got around to getting made. So here it rests for your eyes only. Fun fact–in the short film casting horror writer Martin Lastrapes was to be the guy at the beginning who gets strangled at breakfast! I'm a weird guy, if you're friends with me you may end up dying in a movie...

"ADRA JO CLARK" was in the same manuscript as another short story in this collection, but I felt it could stand alone as something odd. The name of the lead is influenced by girls I had relations with in the past, one of which I had some similar fun in a cemetery with. I'm a pretty weird guy...

"LIBBY" was originally written as a treat for a writer by the name of Libby Grandy, who was President of The Inland Empire branch of The California Writer's Club, which I belonged to. She's an author whose company I enjoy, and I believe she was a little taken aback at first when I shared it with her, but then warmed up after learning that, from a horror writer, this was a gift to be chosen for terrorizing in a tale. We are a strange lot, indeed. It was written circa 2008 and held onto for years until being introduced to Eric Miller at Big Time Books where I adjusted a few parts of the story to "Hollywood" it up for inclusion in *Hell Comes to Hollywood* 2. That included adding the dream ending which I wasn't a big fan of at the time but has grown on me. The full collection went on to be on the preliminary ballot for The Bram Stoker Awards that year.

"NIGHT OF THE NAKED HUNTER"–was painstakingly adapted from a screenplay I co-wrote with Kevin Lahaie, a headlining comedian and fellow fan of all things sleazy horror. Kevin has joined me on so many of my crazy adventures from the professional wrestling-standup comedy TV pilot we were in together, to various tours including performing fully nude at theaters, resorts, and colleges sponsored by The American Association for Nude Recreation. He's always shared my madness, and I love that about him. We tried to get this film funded but never pulled together the complete funds. It broke my heart. I had a nudie resort willing to let us shoot there, a production company willing to shoot it, and some amazing actors including celebrity cameos all lined up. It hurt a lot to not shoot it. So by god, I swear this film will get made one day. It'll be to me what *Evil Dead* was to Sam Raimi or what *Bad Taste* was to Peter Jackson; I get that the premise is wild and outrageous (dare I say Madness?) but THAT'S GOOD because I'm kicking in a door that has been locked to me for too long, I want to scream, "Here's my fully nude, non-sexualized horror film. Let's discuss!" Hopefully it will get some dialogue going about the nature of what truly is obscene. Spoiler alert: It's not your body.

I've also included some Extras that I hope you'll enjoy. I get bored with books that go like this: TITLE–STORY–AUTHOR BIO. I hope you can see I've attempted to be different. If you've enjoyed my Madness please take a moment to review it, tell a friend, and/or maybe consider visiting the publisher's website and signing up to our updates on future releases. If you didn't enjoy the collection or my style, then please just keep your fucking mouth shut.

If there's ever going to be a sequel to this insane collection of pure nuttiness, I plan to feature new works from mostly unpublished writers. I'd like to open the gates for others to get off their ass and take the plunge to see their works in print.

TIM CHIZMAR

After graduating from *Edinboro University of Pennsylvania* with his bachelor's degree in Communications, and obtaining his Master's Degree in Demonology from *Miskotonic University*, Tim Chizmar has written for various magazines, newspapers and websites including *Fangoria*, *First Comics News*, *Girls and Corpses*, and many others. He has sold short stories to such collections as *Chicken Soup for the Soul* and has written various screenplays for Hollywood production companies. Tim is the founder and co-chairman of the Las Vegas chapter of the prestigious *Horror Writers Association*.

Aside from the darker topics, it has not all been a career of terror as his lighter credits to date include *ABC, FOX, Showtime, Playboy, NBC,*

The Hallmark Channel, and many more. He has produced various pilots including in 2010 he developed a comedy/action series for *CMT* with wrestling superstar Rob Van Dam. As a headlining comedian Tim was a favorite at The World-Famous Hollywood IMPROV, The Jon Lovitz Comedy Club, has toured all over the world playing sold-out casinos, clubs and colleges. To date he has worked with such standup legends as Jeff Foxworthy, Gabriel Iglesias, Jon Lovitz, Daniel Tosh, and many others.

When he's not inspiring fellow writers by being on various panels such as San Diego Comic-Con, WonderCon, Scare LA, or speaking at Hollywood Success events, he's constantly working on his next project. Because for Tim Chizmar... There's always a next project! After Tim had been successful enough to become a regular at red carpet premieres, he left all the glitz and glam behind in early 2017 for the mountains of Idaho as he completed this book. He always looks forward to having frank, honest, and engaging discussions on the business of the writing craft with his fellow writers. Tim's advice to young writers is this...

"Be inspired. Are you alive, or are you just breathing?"

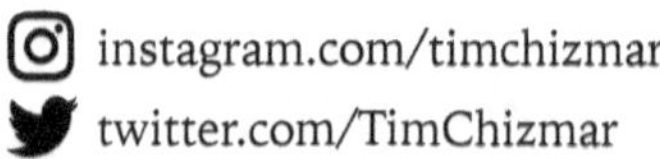

instagram.com/timchizmar

twitter.com/TimChizmar